About the author

At the age of ten Michael Lawrence wanted to be either an archaeologist or an astronomer. Everyone thought he was joking, so instead he went to art school. He's been a graphic designer, a photographer – taking pictures of politicians, pop stars, false teeth and knickers – an antiques dealer and has published a number of children's books.

The Poltergoose started life as a slip of the tongue one breakfast time. Twenty minutes of mad scribbling later, Michael had the bones of the plot, as well as the names of the Three Musketeers, 'Who were already answering back!' he says.

Watch out for more madcap adventures featuring Jiggy, Angie and Pete, in *The Killer Underpants*.

ONE FOR ALL AND ALL FOR LUNCH!

Visit Michael at his website:
www.wordybug.com

A Jiggy McCue Story

The Poltergoose

Michael Lawrence

ORCHARD BOOKS

ORCHARD BOOKS
96 Leonard Street, London EC2A 4XD
Orchard Books Australia
Unit 31/56 O'Riordan Street, Alexandria, NSW 2015
First published in Great Britain in 1999
First paperback publication 2000
Text © Michael Lawrence 1999
Illustrations © Ellis Nadler 1999
The right of Michael Lawrence to be identified as the author, and Ellis
Nadler as the illustrator of this work has been asserted by them in
accordance with the Copyright, Designs and Patents Act, 1988.
A CIP catalogue record for this book is available
from the British Library.
1 84121 107 9 (hardback)
1 86039 836 7 (paperback)
1 3 5 7 9 10 8 6 4 2 (hardback)
13 15 17 19 20 18 16 14 12 (paperback)
Printed in Great Britain

For
David Joby and Adrian Hayes
Old Playmates and School-friends
Good Kids

Chapter one

Listen, don't let's waste any time here. Let's get straight to it. This story is about a dead goose. A dead goose that came back to haunt me. Crazy? You bet. But what can I say? It happened. It happened to me, Jiggy McCue. And my friends Pete Garrett and Angie Mint were witnesses.

An unlikely combination, you might think, two boys and a girl. But Pete and Angie and me, we've known one another since we were just bumps pushing our mothers' clothing out of shape. Best pals, that's us, chums, mates, buds to the last gasp. The Three Musketeers, we call ourselves, even if one of us is a woman. 'One for all, and all for lunch,' we always say. I don't know why.

Now you're probably not wondering why I'm called Jiggy, but I'll tell you anyway. It's because I jig about a lot. Always have. It can come over me any time and there's nothing I can do about it. The Golden Oldies used to think there was something wrong with my nerves. Not so, my nerves are great, they just like to move around a little. I'm probably the only kid whose room you could go into in the middle of the night and find him doing the Cha-Cha in his sleep. Mostly, though, I jig about when I'm excited or nervous, or when I get agitated – like the day my parents told me we were moving from Borderline Way.

It was all Dad's fault. If he hadn't gone and got himself a job at last we'd still have been in the old place and I wouldn't have got myself haunted. My father had been out of work for about five years. He said it was because he knew his worth and wouldn't take just anything. Mum said it was because he's useless.

Anyway, Dad got this job (don't ask me what, it's too boring) and to celebrate he went out and got a new old car to replace the fourteen-year-old heap we used to push round town instead of drive. The new one was only five years old, sort of sky-blue with silver bits that hardly rattled at all, and you didn't have to kick little heaps of rust into the gutter every time you slammed the door, which was nice. We felt like royalty riding round in that car. (Mum even looked a bit like one of the royals, but we didn't tell her, it would have depressed her for days.)

The only trouble with the new car was that it looked all wrong on the curb outside our cruddy old terrace house. Some of the neighbours seemed to think so too, and when Dad had replaced the hub-caps and windscreen wipers for the third time, and sprayed over 'Rich sod' in a slightly different blue, he and Mum started talking about a new house to go with the car while it was still in one piece.

So they bought a house on the Brook Farm Estate. The house where all my troubles started.

Chapter Two

The Brook Farm Estate is called the Brook Farm Estate because it's built on the place where Brook Farm used to be. Clever, eh? There's no sign of the farm now, it's all bright new houses with half-finished gardens, but back when it was still a farm Pete and Angie and I used to do odd jobs there during the summer holidays – collecting eggs, raking up cow muck, all the usual barmy farmy stuff. The farmer, Mr Brook, old Brooky, he didn't pay much and he wasn't that keen on kids, but we sort of liked going there because it was so open and all, and there weren't wheely bins and walls with bad wallpaper wherever you looked.

But then the miserable old devil spoiled everything. He retired. Sold the farm to a building firm and this new estate and shopping centre started to go up. When we moved in only about half the houses were built and the roads were still being laid and nothing much had been vandalised yet and it felt all wrong. The new house was a palace compared to the old one, but I didn't like it at first. Didn't really want to like it. Pete and Angie came over quite often, but it wasn't like the old days when they just wandered through the gap in the fence when they felt like it. They thought the new place was cool. Envied me, they said.

'Yeah, but it's not like *home*, is it?' I said.

'That's what's so good about it,' said Ange.

We'd been in the new house about three weeks when Mum and Dad decided it should have a name. I wasn't keen. We'd always been able to find our house on Borderline Way without calling its name. I mentioned this.

'The house on Borderline Way was just the place we lived in,' Mum said. 'This one's different. It's special. It deserves a name.'

'I like the number,' I said. 'I think it's a terrific number.'

'What's so terrific about 23?' Dad said.

'I don't know, it just…has something.'

'We'll still keep the number,' Mum said. 'But a name will give the place an identity. Set it apart from all the others.'

'We've each put half a dozen in the hat,' Dad said. He shook his horrible *Help the Aged* bobble hat in my face. 'Thought we'd see what came up. Let fate decide.'

'Fate?' I cried. 'Fate? Have you any idea what fate can *do* to people?'

They just grinned, and suddenly I was very nervous. That hat could be stuffed with the kind of names I'd never live down. I leant against something to stop my knees shaking. I think it was Stallone, our cat, because something scratched my behind and it wasn't me.

'Tell you what,' Mum said, 'to make it fair why don't you put some names in too?'

Now this was a surprise. 'You'd trust me to name our house?'

'Course we would,' Mum said. 'Wouldn't we, Mel?'

Blind panic stamped itself on Dad's face for a minute, but then he took a deep breath, cleared his throat, said, 'Course we would,' and reached for Mum's hand to give it a little squeeze. He'd been doing that a lot since we moved and it was starting to make me twitch.

'And whichever one comes out is the one we use?' I said. 'Even if it's my choice?'

'Of course!' they chortled like a pair of happy maniacs.

'All right then.' I reached for a pad and wrote down six names, right off the top of my head. They were going to regret this.

I folded my bits of paper and dropped them in the bobble hat. Dad shook them all up and Mum said: 'Who's going to choose?'

'It shouldn't be one of us,' I said. 'We don't want to get the blame.'

'Well there's no one else,' Dad said.

'There's no rush. Why don't we just wait till someone knocks on the door? They can pick it out for us.'

There was a knock on the door.

'Bingo!' Dad yelled.

It was Pete and Angie. I could have killed them.

We told them about the house name deal and they said cool and I said you're out of your minds, and they tossed for it to decide which of them was going to be the one to ruin my life. Pete won, and he gave me the evil eye as he stuck his mitt in the

Help the Aged hat.

I suppose I shouldn't complain. At least the name that came out was one of mine. But when Pete read it out I said, 'No, no, do it again. That one was meant as a joke.'

'No, Jig,' Dad said. 'We made an agreement. Whatever came out of the hat was the one we'd use.' He smirked at Mum, who smirked back. '*The Dorks* it is then – agreed?'

Chapter Three

My parents are aliens. They're from another planet. Got to be. I mean normal people, human beings from planet Earth, they'd say, 'Yeah, real scream, kid,' and change the subject till everyone forgot about house names. But not them. Oh no. They go right out and pay somebody to paint *The Dorks* on a bit of wood with flowers round it, then screw it to the wall by the front door for all the world to point at and tell their friends. Sometimes, after the sign went up, there'd be someone on the step trying to sell us something we didn't want, like dusters or religion, and you could see it was all they could do to keep from sinking to their knees with a hanky in their mouth. Embarrassing? I still go out with a blanket over my head.

Apart from the name it wasn't as bad at *The Dorks* as I thought it would be. For one thing the toilet flushed every time. That made a real change, believe me. And for the first time ever we had a built-in electric cooker which didn't blow all the fuses in the house whenever you boiled an egg. We had the same old junk furniture, but at least Dad and I could put our muddy feet up on that.

The most important room in the house of course was my bedroom. It wasn't like my comfortable old room at Borderline Way – it was neat, it was clean, tidy, even smelled nice, but I soon put that right. It was here, in my new room, that it all started.

The first thing that happened was Roger falling off his hook. Roger's my gorilla. I've had him since I was little when Dad brought him home one Christmas. He was drunk. Dad, that is, not Roger (Roger doesn't drink, he's a toy). Roger has these very long thin arms and these palms which stick together when they touch. What you do is you loop his arms round something and join his hands so that he hangs from whatever it is. Like a big plastic hook.

Well there's Roger hanging from the big plastic hook I've got fixed to my wall and there's me sitting on my bed daydreaming about putting chewing gum on my most hated teacher's chair or something, and I must have been vaguely looking in Roger's direction because when his hands suddenly flew apart and he fell to the floor I jumped so high my head almost cracked the ceiling.

'You stupid gorilla!' I yelled, storming over. 'You almost gave me a heart attack!' Roger didn't reply. I picked him up. 'Nothing to say for yourself, eh?' I hammered his head against the wall a few times. 'One more trick like that and you're a rug!'

As I was fixing his hands together again — behind his back as a punishment — there was this crash. I spun round but I was too late to see it, so I could only guess what happened. My guess was this: my pillow, which I'd been leaning on a second before, had lifted off the bed, flown across the room, and slammed into my toy rocking-horse shelf.

I'll tell you about my toy rocking-horses. Mum had been collecting them for me since before I was born. She seemed to have got it into her head that I wanted the entire world supply of the things. I had about sixty by this time, all standing there facing the same way like an army of rocking-horse impressionists looking for a life, all sizes from so small they could fit in an eggcup to big enough to hold in two hands. Some of them were made of plastic, some of china, some of papier mâché, some of wood. Every birthday, every Christmas, every excuse, my collection was added to. Not only did I always know I was going to get another one (sometimes a whole family of them) but I could tell they were rocking-horses even before I unwrapped them. It wasn't difficult. Wrapping paper does not a disguise make, not for rocking-horses.

'Wow, thanks, Mum,' I'd say, all bright-eyed with surprise and gratitude. 'Thanks, Dad.'

'Don't thank me,' Dad would mutter. 'Last thing I'd give you is another bloody rocking-horse.'

This was the lifetime's collection of unwanted rocking-horses that my pillow flew at and scattered all by itself. All I could do was stand there gulping silently. My mother was just along the landing doing something with a duster. She heard the crash, stuck her head round the door just in time to stop silent gulping becoming a hobby.

'Jiggy, what on earth was...?' Then she saw. 'Oh!'

She came in, fell to her knees, stared about her at

the Great Rocking-Horse Disaster.

'Oh Jiggy,' she said, and 'Oh Jiggy' and 'Oh, Jiggy, Jiggy, Jiggy,' until I finally remembered my name.

'Don't blame me,' were my first words after my hair stopped standing on end. 'It was my pillow, it just sort of…knocked them down.'

Mum glared up at me. 'Oh. I see. Your pillow. And you didn't happen to be swinging it round the room at the time, I suppose.'

Now this got to me. I mean I could see the way it looked, but I don't like being accused of things I haven't done.

'If you must know,' I said, 'I was over there banging Roger's head against the wall. If that makes the walls vibrate and sends pillows and rocking-horses flying, well all I can say is it's a pretty feeble excuse for a house we have here.'

'Oh look,' she said, obviously not hanging on every word, 'two of the most delicate ones are…' She reached for a couple of glass twins. Ex-glass twins. Now they were glass quads. 'These were my favourites,' she wailed. 'Jiggy, how could you, how *could* you?'

I felt myself go hot under the collar. What do you

25

have to do to get through to some people?

'I'll say it again,' I said. 'I did not do this. Do you want subtitles for the hard of hearing? Do I have to get someone to stand at the side of the room speaking in sign language? Look. Read my lips. I – am – not – guilty!'

Bad move. The old girl went red in the face. Bug-eyed.

'Don't you *dare* talk to me like that, young man!'

But I was up and running now. Mouth open and flapping.

'I mean, yeah, right, sometimes I want to jump on rocking-horses till they rock no more. Some mornings I have this fierce desire to throw the whole lot out of the window and watch traffic drive over them till lunchtime. *But I am not the Brook Farm Rocking-Horse Killer!*'

Somewhere in all this a big change came over her. She went all sort of saggy and sad. Her forehead became one big crease and her mouth went down at the corners. Suddenly my 37-year-old mother was a hundred and five.

'I thought you liked them,' she said in this quiet little disappointed voice that grabs your heart and wrings it out like a wet sock. 'I really thought you liked them.'

Then she jumped up and ran out of the room with her knuckles in her mouth.

I felt bad. So bad I forgot to be miffed that she didn't believe me. It must have hurt, hearing my real feelings about the rocking-horses after all this time. I should have told her years ago. Got it all out of the way right off. My first words shouldn't have been 'Mum-mum, Dad-dad.' They should have been 'No lousy rocking-horses!' Then there'd have been none of this.

Chapter Four

When I got home from school next day all the rocking-horses had disappeared. In their place was this bowl of white plastic flowers that a hand grenade couldn't destroy. That made me feel even worse. What had she done with the rocking-horses? I couldn't ask. And you know, I sort of missed them now they weren't there any more. I'd grown up with them after all, they'd rocked with me from the cradle, always been there whether I wanted them or not.

It was three days after the rocking-horse incident that the next thing happened.

I was in bed reading a horror story under the duvet by torchlight (the only way to read them) when suddenly...

Picture the scene. I'd just got to the bit where the two kids – Sam and Roddy – are pushing back the huge front door of this dark old house on the hill. They're there looking for their mysteriously missing friends and of course there's this storm going like the clappers – thunder, lightning, high winds, the works. Well Sam and Roddy push open the creaking door and there they are in this massive old dark old hall, which is very, very, *very* eerie. Suddenly the door slams behind them and the bolts are drawn across by this invisible hand, and there's this terrifying wailing sound, and then...

And then the duvet lifts off me, floats up to the ceiling, and winds itself round the Chinese paper lampshade.

'AAAAAARRRRRGGGH!' I said, or something quite like it.

While this was still bouncing round the walls collecting an echo, I heard Mum and Dad coming at the run from different directions, Dad taking the stairs four at a time, Mum shooting out of the bathroom. They were still on their way when the duvet yanked at the lampshade like it had a life of its own – yanked so hard there was a flash and the light came down, shade, bulb, the lot. I stared at the twitching, sparking wires in the ceiling and the burst duvet floating carpetward accompanied by a shower of white feathers. The duvet came to rest on the floor a split second before the Golden Oldies fell in, all wild-eyed and vocal.

Naturally, the first thing they did was flick the light switch up and down a few thousand times, *click-click*, *click-click*, *click-click*, before realising it was kaput. Silhouetted dramatically in the landing light, they took in the dangling wires. From the dangling wires they looked at me with the pillow in my teeth. Then back at the ceiling. Then back at me. A passing stranger would have thought they were into vertical tennis.

I jumped off the bed and ran to them. There are times in a kid's life when he has to make use of his parents or they might as well not be there. My head was already deep in Mum's chest before I realised it was not only wet but mostly nude as she'd just jumped out of the bath and pulled her dressing-gown on to get to me without delay. I shuddered, pushed both bits of wet chest away, and threw myself at Dad instead. And you know what he did? He pushed *me* away, held me at arm's length by the shoulders, saying heavy manful things like: 'Jiggy, what is all this?' and 'What have you been up to here?' and 'What

30

happened to the light?' Questions, questions, when all I wanted was a decent hug and someone to say 'There, there, son, it's all right, you put your thumb in your mouth and I'll make you some hot chocolate and read you the Noddy book I've been saving for emergencies like this.'

Once I'd calmed down I explained what had happened, but I needn't have bothered. They thought I'd yanked the light down myself. And when they saw my horror novel they looked at one another, sighed knowingly, and confiscated it. Then they left, muttering stuff about not knowing what had got into me lately. And me? Did they give any thought to me? Did it so much as tiptoe across their tiny minds that I might be a bit upset about something? What do you think? I was left sitting there all alone on the side of the bed shaking and wet (part sweat, part Mum's chest), waiting for the duvet on the floor to move again. It didn't, and eventually I felt safe enough to crawl under the bed and attempt a spot of shut-eye, cuddling my slippers.

I didn't make it to dreamland. A sort of hiss jerked my eyelids back. I peered out from under

the bed. The door was still open and the landing
light was still on, which meant I could just make
out the feathers from the duvet doing a little dance
in mid-air. This time I didn't yell. I was all out of
yell. I shot out from under the bed, threw myself
across the room and along the landing, straight
into Mum and Dad's room. Dad was just getting
into his pyjamas and I gave him such a shock that
he fell on the bed with his bare bott in the air.

'Dad! You've got to see this!'

'Oh, give it a *rest*, Jiggy!' he said, trying to sort
himself out and recover his dignity.

'Go back to bed, darling,' Mum said. 'Enough's
enough now.'

And that was it. I know them when they're in
that sort of mood. Nothing will make them listen.
So I gave up. Went downstairs. Spent the rest of the
night scrunched up on the couch, shivering. I kept
the light on. Didn't sleep a wink.

Chapter Five

I hadn't told Pete and Angie about the Great Rocking-Horse Massacre. I thought they might have a bit of a problem with it. 'Hey, you two, guess what happened to me last night, there I am sitting in my room minding my own business and my pillow throws itself at my rocking-horses, whaddayasay to *that*?' What they'd have said to that was 'Yeah Jig, fascinating, out of this world, come with us, they say the new doc down at the med centre's a whiz with raving lunatics.'

But now too much was happening to keep it all to myself. I had to share it with someone, and they were my best friends, so I told them – about the rocking-horses, the duvet snatching the light, the dancing feathers – and of course they covered their mouths and skewered their fingers at their heads, so I said 'OK, come to my house, I'll show you,' which wasn't very bright seeing as there didn't seem to be a pattern to any of this. I mean, like,

33

why should something happen just because I'd organised seating arrangements?

Mum and Dad were both still out at work when we got to my place after school, but Pete and Angie rang their folks to let them know where they were. This was a one call operation. I should mention that although all three of us happen to be from one child families, Pete and Ange are also from one *parent* families these days. I won't go into what happened to her father and his mother or we'll be here all day, but the thing is that Pete and his dad Oliver had just moved in with Angie and her mum Audrey. To save on the gas bills, Oliver said. They must think we're stupid.

Up in my room we waited for the best part of an hour for something to happen. Then Pete said: 'I think you dreamed it.'

'If I'd dreamed it,' I snapped, 'Mum and Dad wouldn't have been so uptight, and I'd still have floor-to-ceiling rocking-horses and a light.'

Angie looked up at the naked wires. 'Is your dad going to fix that?'

'I doubt it,' I said. 'He doesn't like messing with electricity. Doesn't even change bulbs if he can get someone else to do it.'

'So what happens exactly?' Pete said.

'Mum does it. Or I do.'

'No, I mean with this stuff flying about.'

I slapped my forehead. How many times did I have to go over this? 'How many times do I have to go over this?' I said.

'Yeah, well, it seems pretty funny that it only happens when there's nobody around but you.'

'I can't help that, I'm just the unhappy victim.'

'Hmm,' said Angie Mint.

We both looked at her. Her eyes were all screwed up and she was stroking the beard she didn't have.

'Hmm what?' I said.

'If you didn't dream it or imagine it, if it all really happened the way you say it did, it sounds like you've got yourself a poltergeist.'

Pete smirked. 'Poltergeist? As in ghost?'

'As in *mischievous* ghost. One that chucks things about and makes a general nuisance of itself.'

'Sounds like me according to my dad,' I said.

'There was this programme on telly about them the other night,' Angie said.

'I didn't see it,' said Pete.

35

'You were playing your Road Rage computer game.'

'What sort of things do they do?' I asked her.

'Oh, silly little things. Childish things, like...' She looked around for an example and fixed on the framed poster of some dolphins that Mum had hung above my bed because she likes dolphins. 'Like making pictures fall off walls.'

The picture fell off the wall.

I peered through the dust kicked up by four Musketeer heels galloping across the room and down the stairs. The front door was still rocking on its hinges as it became clear that this was only the beginning; that 'it' had just been waiting to get me alone, and now that we were...

For starters it whipped up the duvet and threw it over me so I had to fight to get out of it, which wasn't very easy. If you want to know the truth, it was like being held in the grip of a...well, a duvet. But when I was free I made a run for it, like Pete and Angie before me, though I didn't make it out of the house like they did. Furthest I got was the landing, then there was this hiss, followed by this flapping sound, and next thing I know my legs are being attacked by something sharp and pointy and unfriendly. I ran into the bathroom, slammed the door behind me, turned the key. I was safe. Terrified, speechless, line dancing with the loofah – but safe.

Or so I thought.

SSSSSSsssssSSssssSSSSSSsssss

It was in there with me! In the bathroom, jabbing at the toilet seat of all things, lifting it up, letting it fall, lifting it up, letting it – well, you get the idea. I reached behind me for the door key. My fingers didn't seem to want to work and the key dropped to the floor. I slithered down the door, fumbling about for the key. While I was doing this, the hissing flapping invisible thing found my dad's talcum powder. Talcum powder which, as usual, Dad hadn't closed properly to block off the little holes on top. And now, because of my father's *carelessness*, it was suddenly snowing talc that smelt of 'woodspice with extract of birchwood', whatever that is. In seconds the bathroom was covered in the stuff. So was I. I could hardly see for extract of birchwood, let alone woodspice. My only consolation was that I smelt gorgeous.

Half blind, half delirious, half wetting myself, I snatched up the key, found the keyhole, turned the key, flung back the door, and –

SSSSSSsssssssSsssssSSSSSSsssss

flap-flap-flap-flap-flap-flap-flap-flap

YYYAAAAAAAAHHHHHhhhhhhhh

The last of these was me going down the banister one-handed, no feet, hissed at and flapped at and pecked at from behind. All this might have been easier to handle if I could have seen what was pecking on me, but I couldn't. Not then. I didn't get to see it till I made it to the living room. I'd just jumped on the couch and was about to plunge my head in one of Mum's big cushions, when the talcum powder snowstorm that had followed me in took on a shape.

The shape of a goose. A big goose. A big *angry* goose.

And then the talc was shooting off in all directions and the goose was trying to get at me through the cushion, and in a jiff the stuffing was

38

on the outside and I'm standing there with an empty cover. I threw it away, dived under the coffee table – and discovered that it already had a resident, Stallone the cat, scared out of his fur by the thing that was after me. So there I was with my head under a coffee table while an invisible goose remodelled my back-end as a tea strainer and a demented cat tried to scratch my eyes out. Let me tell you, it was not a good position to be in.

Then, without warning, all this gratuitous violence stopped. The room went quiet, the goose stopped pecking me, and Stallone slipped away to do what he does best, which is lick like a madman between his hind legs.

My mother had come home.

She entered the room just as I was backing out of the coffee table. I saw her jaw hit the carpet as she took in a room that had not previously been covered in woodspice with extract of birchwood.

'Jiggy McCue!' she shrieked. 'What have you been doing *now*!?'

Chapter Six

My mother absolutely refused to believe it wasn't me that had covered the house with talcum powder and shredded the cushion – not even when I told her I was being haunted by a goose. Her nose was still a bit in the air next morning when she handed me the big soft parcel tied up with string that arrived just before school, though she hung about to see what it was. It was something I'd have given one of my dad's arms not to receive. A hand-knitted sweater from my gran.

'It's not my birthday,' I said, gaping at it in disbelief.

Mum's eyes had a hard time staying in their sockets too. She tried to focus on the scratchy little note that came with it.

'It says here that even though she never sees you and she may not last much longer seeing as nobody cares about her, she wants you to know that she's thinking of you.' She looked at the sweater again, and flinched. 'You must write and…thank her.'

She held it against my chest. It was bright blue with my name on the front. The sweater, not the chest. The letters were luminous orange and as big as a house. My name just hung there, stretching from armpit to armpit like an axe murderer's grin.

'Thank her?' I said. 'I'm thinking of sending her hate mail.'

When I went up to clean my teeth I kicked the sweater under my bed to fade quietly from living memory. Then I decided to have a stab at getting Dad on my side about the goose and talcum powder thing. You never know with Dad. Sometimes you can get through to him. Not often, because he doesn't usually listen, but sometimes.

He'd gone down the garden to look at his Rodadoodah bush. Our back garden is sort of L-shaped, and the bottom part is hidden from the house by a high fence. Dad's patch is round there, out of sight. He hates gardening more than anything except cleaning windows and cars, but he'd been going down there to check out the Rodadoodah on the hour ever since the big trip to the garden centre the Sunday before. They'd gone

41

there to get things for this rockery Mum had been planning. She bought a lot of other stuff besides and planted most of it herself while Dad, worn out from driving ten minutes each way and carrying plants in, got a beer out of the fridge and read the paper. But she deliberately left a couple of things for him. 'It's your garden too, Mel,' she said. 'Perhaps you'd care to do something towards it...?' Which meant that he'd better if he knew what was good for him.

So Dad read the instructions tied to the leg of the Rodadoodah bush, dug a hole out of sight of the house, and dropped it in. But here's the thing: the following morning it was still alive! He couldn't believe it. Everything he'd ever planted had immediately committed suicide, and here was this Rodadoodah in bloom already. All right, it had been like that when they bought it, but that isn't the point. The point is that the dinky little pink flowers stuck all over it hadn't fallen off when he planted it and they hadn't fallen off the next day, and here they were, still in place three days later. It looked like all he had to do now was pray for rain occasionally.

'Hey Jig! Am I a gardener or am I a gardener?'

'You want to be careful,' I warned him. 'Get it right once and she'll have you out here all the time – even Saturday afternoons.'

I saw him go pale. Saturday afternoons were sacred to him. They were football-on-telly times, jump-about-on-the-couch-and-punch-the-air times. 'You might have something there,' he said, a frown dashing across his brow dribbling a ball of sweat.

'Don't worry. If it comes to it I'll sneak out one night and kill it for you.'

He looked relieved. 'Thanks, son.'

'Dad?' I said. 'What would you say if I said I was being haunted by a goose?'

'Is this a riddle?'

'No, straight question.'

'I'd probably say you're quackers.'

'That's ducks,' I said. 'This is a goose.'

'Oh,' he said, and his eyes glazed over. I'd lost him.

Chapter Seven

Before the Golden Oldies bundled me out of Borderline Way against my will, Pete, Angie and I always walked to school together, but now that I live on the Brook Farm Estate I have to come from a different direction, so our paths don't cross. The way I go takes me through the new shopping centre. That morning, like every morning, kids were swarming across the square, yelling, kicking squashed cans about, cracking one another round the head with their bags, all the usual.

There were some men in the square putting up video cameras, four cameras, one on each side. There'd been so much vandalism in the shopping centre since it was finished six months ago that it was already starting to look like it had been brought over by the Romans. There was this big campaign going on to catch the Brook Farm Vandals, as the local paper called them. Some people wanted them behind bars, others wanted them sent bungy-jumping without a bit of elastic. The cameras the men were putting up were big jobs, the kind you can't miss blindfolded on a dark night. Dad says they'd decided on cameras like that instead of neat little itty-bitty spy things tucked out of sight because no one in his right mind would vandalise things if he *knew* he was being watched.

I met Pete and Angie in our usual corner of the school playground and told them my news.

'A ghost *goose*?' Pete said. 'You're pulling my beak.'

'It's true, every word. Would I lie to you?'

He pulled open his sleeve and laughed down it. I sighed, and turned to Angie, expecting more of the same. But no, she was looking quite serious – and over her shoulder.

'I believe you,' she said. 'After yesterday I'd believe you if you said it was a ghost rhinoceros.'

'Angie, a picture got fed up of hanging around on a wall,' Pete said. 'Big deal.'

'Big enough to send you flying down the stairs head first,' I reminded him.

'I over-reacted.' He eyed Angie. 'We both did.'

But Angie wasn't having this. 'You were sick with terror. You couldn't eat your tea, wouldn't talk to anyone, went to bed early with a hot water bottle even though it was a warm night. Mum and Oliver wondered if you were coming down with something.'

'What I was coming down with was common sense,' Pete said, all superior.

'Ha!' said Angie.

'You don't really believe all this stuff. You can't. Jiggy's putting us on, has to be.'

He looked as ruffled as a bad haircut. I don't think he expected Angie to take my side. All our lives we never went in for side-taking. We'd always been like that – you know – us against the world, one for all and all for lunch. But now that sides were coming up for grabs, Pete obviously thought Angie would be on his.

'If Jiggy says there's a ghost goose in his house,' Angie said, 'there's a ghost goose in his house.'

I tell you, if she hadn't been one of my best mates I'd have thrown my arms round her and kissed her.

'You must be going soft,' Pete said to her. 'Going all *girly* on us all of a sudden.'

46

Angie stiffened. Narrowed her eyes. She put her nose against his. Grabbed his shirt. 'What did you say?'

Pete knew he'd made a mistake. Angie has been a tough cookie from the day she gave up rusks. He shuffled his feet like two playing cards who've been kicked out of the pack for cheating.

'Just a figure of speech, Ange. Mind the shirt, huh?'

She put him down. I said to her (just her, Pete could do what he liked), I said: 'And I had the weirdest feeling coming to school. Like I was being followed.'

'Don't tell me.' Pete's smirk was back in place, and it was awfully high on the Punch Me scale. 'By a dead goose.'

'Well yes, *actually*,' I replied.

'Heeeeey, is that the time?' He raised his wrist and looked at the watch he wasn't wearing. 'Gotta run. Urgent business in Sane Land.'

And he ran off across the playground to kick a ball about with a bunch of lowheads he would normally swim rivers to avoid.

'Don't mind him,' Angie said.

47

'What about you? How do I know you're not just setting me up for the big put-down?'

Ange looked offended. 'Jiggy McCue, how long have we known one another?'

'Since we were no-high,' I said.

'So do me the courtesy of believing me when I say I believe *you*, all right? Now. Tell me everything.'

I told her everything. About the duvet throwing itself over me, about being chased along the landing and down the stairs, about seeing a goose's outline in woodspice with extract of birchwood, about Mum thinking even *that* mess was down to me.

'And you think it followed you to school?'

'I might have imagined that. It might just be getting to me. I kept thinking I heard this sort of…hiss.'

'Hiss?'

'Geese do that. Remember old Brooky's goose? Chased us for miles just for setting foot in the yard once.'

Angie nodded. 'Scary old bird. Brooky called it his guard goose. Didn't need a dog with her around, he said.'

SSSSSSsssssssSsssssSSSsssss

We jumped three metres in the air, clutching at one another. '*Where did that come from*?!' Angie rasped as we came down.

Some of the nearest kids were looking at us. Bryan Ryan shouted over. 'McCue bothering you, Minty?'

'Get lost, Bry-Ry!' Angie shouted back.

'Yeah, get lost, Bry-Ry,' I repeated. Ryan shrugged and turned away.

Angie reached out and patted the air nervously. 'Can't feel anything.'

'You wouldn't, it's a ghost.'

'You said you felt it when it chased you. Your legs, your bum.'

'That's true.' I started patting the air too.

'Lookit them two,' Eejit Atkins said a little way off. 'Whacha doin', pr'tendin' t' be blind or sumfin'?'

'No,' I said, 'we're pretending to be stupid. We're doing Eejit Atkins impressions.'

'You wanna watch it, McCue. Less you wanna fump.'

And he walked off with his idiot buds, all rolling their shoulders, knuckles dragging the tarmac.

The bell rang. The bell rang and there was this startled flurrying noise close by.

'What was that?' Angie said.

'The bell,' I said.

'No, the sound like flapping wings.'

'Wings flapping,' I said.

'What say we get outta here?'

'I say terrific,' I said as my feet hit the playground at speed.

Angie was at my side as we pushed through others less keen to get to class than us.

'Oi!'

'Watch 'oo yer pushin'!'

'Wossup wi' them two anyaah?'

And then there were other shouts, panicky sort of shouts, way behind us as we made it to the main building.

The goose, the ghost goose, flapping and hissing its way through the crowd, was coming after us.

Chapter Eight

Face-Ache Dakin, our form tutor, isn't exactly what you'd call popular. He picks on you for nothing and is never happier than when he's handing out detentions and stuff. One of the kids who gets the worst treatment from him is his own son, Milo. I suppose he picks on Milo for the sake of it so as not to show favouritism, but on a good day Milo gives as good as he gets, which always goes down well with the class. He did even better than usual the morning Angie and I shook off the ghost goose in the playground. It was just after registration, and we were getting our things out for one of Face-Ache's boring, boring, *boring* maths lessons.

'You, boy, stop talking,' growls Dakin.

'I wasn't talking, Dad,' replies Milo, then grins all round. 'Sorry, I mean *Sir.*'

'One hundred lines by tomorrow morning!'

'What for?' says Milo.

'For answering back.'

'Oh, I thought it was for lying – which I wasn't, as you know.'

'Careful, laddie, or it'll be two hundred.'

'Sorry, can't do any lines tonight,' Milo says. 'Busy-busy.'

'What? What's that you say?'

'My turn for cooking and washing-up duty.' He turns to the class. 'Since my mum ran off with a jogger, we take things in turns.' He flips back to Daddy. 'Beans and chips OK tonight, Pop?'

'Stand up!' screams his doting father in this strangled voice.

'Righto.' Milo gets up, hands in pockets.

'And take your hands out of your pockets!'

Milo takes his hands out of his pockets – and gets to work on his nose. I mean really gets to work. I don't know how he does it, probably a bit of string from his pocket, but he tugs this stuff out of one of his nostrils, tugs and tugs until it's about the length of his arm, like super snot. Even curls his tongue up to lick it as it goes by.

The class is having a hard time controlling its joy by this time, but Face-Ache is not so happy. He storms up to Milo's desk and leans over him, neck out like a spring.

'Young man, you will see me after school.'

He says this in such a way that you know, you just know, that he's forgotten for a minute that this kid is his own flesh and blood.

Milo hasn't. 'I will anyway,' he chirps. 'You're driving me home. As well as up the wall,' he adds, just loud enough for the whole class to catch. By now it's all we can do not to roll in the aisles with our legs in the air.

'Sit down! I will deal with you *later*!'

Milo sits. There's a halo over his head. His father returns to his desk and leans on it with his fists clenched, glowering round at us, daring us to so much as titter behind our hands. He takes several deep slow breaths, then snaps suddenly to attention.

'I shall return in one minute! And I don't want to hear a sound in this room while I'm gone! Not a *murmur*, d'you hear me?'

He attacks the door, flings it back so hard it bounces, then slams it after him, rattling the roof. It's my guess he has to go and do some serious damage to the bike sheds, but whatever the reason, his absence gives the class time to collapse in grateful hysteria and give Milo a standing ovation and offers of money to teach us how to do that and get away with it.

It was while Face-Ache was away trying to keep his head from detonating that an even more memorable kind of hell broke loose.

It started with a hiss.

The first hiss was quieter than the noise of everyone getting out of their skulls, and Angie and I were the only ones to hear it, probably because we were half expecting it. Even Pete didn't hear it, though he actually sits nearer to me than Angie, right next to me in fact. In any case, Pete wasn't sitting now, he was standing on his desk making rude signs at the door old Face-Ache had just gone through. But he sure felt it when he got beaked. Another word for that might be goosed, of course, which means that Pete got either beaked by a goose or goosed by a beak, depending how you look at it.

Anyway, he gave a yell and fell off his desk, and when he got up he was clutching his backside and glaring at me.

'Did you do that?'

I had no intention of answering this. Also, there were other things to think about than Pete's rear end. Like the shouts of terror from across the room as six or seven kids started running round in circles followed by this great flapping noise as the invisible ghost goose chased them, hissing and pecking, pecking and hissing.

Fear spread through the class like wildfire. Before, there was just the cheerful noise of a roomful of kids celebrating the temporary departure of a teacher they didn't like. Now it was the panic of a roomful of kids being attacked by something big and angry that they couldn't see. I noticed that Pete's mouth had fallen open. It was trying to find words. It found two. They were: 'It's true!'

Now in an odd sort of way I felt responsible for all this. For some reason the ghost goose had decided to haunt me, and because it was haunting me it had followed me to school, and because it had followed me to school it was now attacking my classmates. Whether I wanted it or not it was my ghost and I couldn't just stand there and watch it go after the other kids.

I tore a curtain down from one of the windows.

The curtain was orange, but that's probably not important. I stalked the empty space where the goose seemed to be. Tossed the curtain. It fell to the ground, empty. The goose had moved on. Now it was terrorising another batch.

I changed direction. Round and round the room I went, curtain held out before me, not even sure if you *can* capture a ghost with a curtain, even an orange one. Every time I thought I was close enough to run a test on this the goose swerved and left me with a curtain full of air. It wasn't hard to tell where it was because that was where things were flying around and kids were reeling and yelling and treading on one another's faces. There was hardly a desk left standing now. Our beloved classroom was rapidly losing popularity as a place to be. Kids were fighting one another to get out the door.

Somewhere in all this I heard Angie's voice. 'I'll go and find Face-Ache!' Then Pete's. 'I'll come with you! Hang on in there, Jig!'

And suddenly the door was closed and the goose and I were alone.

I climbed over a couple of wrecked desks and

several chairs, slowly, cautiously. The goose – still hissing and flapping invisibly, but less frantically now – moved ahead of me. It was over by the door now. I got closer. Closer, closer, curtain at the ready.

The door opened.

'Oh no you don't!' I cried, and leapt into action. I threw the curtain, then jumped after it, brought it crashing to the ground and put all my weight on it. It was moving under me but it wasn't getting away now.

I'd done it! I'd got it! You *could* catch a ghost!

There was a muffled voice. A muffled angry voice. Not a goose's voice, which was a bit of a puzzle as it was coming from inside the curtain I was sitting on. It was saying something odd too. Something that sounded awfully like: 'McCue, I'm going to have your guts for garters for this!'

I got off the curtain. Looked under it. Face-Ache Dakin glared up at me with eyes like burning coals.

'Sir,' I said. 'Listen, I can explain everything...'

57

Chapter Nine

That night, while Dad hung about on the landing pretending he wasn't there, Mum sat me down quietly on my bed and told me that she was taking me to a behavioural psychologist. 'A behavioural psychologist,' she told me, 'is someone who tries to work out why a person does the things he does.'

I said: 'So why don't you take Dad to one?'

'Hey, don't bring me into this,' Dad said from the landing, blowing his cover without any trouble.

'Why would I take your father to a behavioural psychologist?'

'The way he carries on when he's watching football?'

'We don't need to take your father anywhere to know why he behaves like that. He behaves like that because he's never grown up.'

'Well neither have I,' I said. 'And I have an excuse.'

But there was nothing I could say. They'd made

up their minds. My parents were taking me to a shrink. They were going to have me shrink-wrapped.

Mum kept me off school the day of the appointment and we took the bus to town and walked to this old building full of offices where Serious People worked. The name on the door we ended up at had the name Dr Edward Pickett on it, with all these capital letters after it that didn't make any sense.

We'd been sitting in the waiting room for about fifteen minutes when this tall thin gent appeared, said 'Good morning!' in an unnaturally hearty voice, and held open his office door. I took the hint and went in. As the door closed behind me I knew that Mum was already reaching for the first *Hello!* magazine.

It wasn't a very interesting office. It had some shelves with some fat books on, and a small neat desk over in one corner with a computer, and there were some filing cabinets and two red leather armchairs facing one another. The walls were covered with these big pointless paintings, all blobs and bits of colour that looked like they'd been slapped on with a mop or lobbed with a spoon.

The tall thin gent introduced himself as Dr Pickett (surprise, surprise) and pointed to one of the red leather armchairs. This chair was in the middle of the room, while the one he bagged for himself had its back to the wall, right under the biggest, most pointless painting of all. We both sat down and I tried not to stare at his hair, which believe me wasn't easy. The doc's hair seemed to end just above his ears, but on one side he had grown it so long that it would have touched his shoulder if he'd just let it fall naturally. Instead, he swept it up across his hairless roof, up and over, till it joined the other sad little batch cringing round the opposite ear. He must have oiled this long hair or something because it just lay there on top of his skull, glistening. I wanted to ask him a question. I wanted to say: 'Hey, Pickett, explain to me why an expert in the way people behave tries to con us he isn't as bald as a boiled egg.' I didn't, of course.

'Make yourself comfortable, er...Jiggy,' he said, glancing at some notes on a small table beside his chair. I made myself comfortable. 'Now I want you to understand that there's nothing to worry about here. We're just going to have a little chat about things. There's nothing to be concerned about.'

'I'm not concerned,' I said. I didn't tell him that I was more annoyed than anything. Annoyed that no one believed me when I said I didn't do things.

'For someone who's not concerned,' the doc said, 'you seem to be having some difficulty keeping still.'

'Oh, that's just me. I always jig about. Always have. That's why I'm called Jiggy.'

'Ah.'

He raised his hand to his face and spoke into it, so quietly I couldn't hear what he was saying. I felt I shouldn't be listening anyway. This was a personal conversation between him and his hand. While he was talking to his hand my eyes drifted to the picture over his head. It was one of those pictures you couldn't ignore if you wanted to. Pickett caught me looking at this and got kind of excited. It all began to make sense. He sat there under that picture and you sat opposite him, and every time you looked at it because you couldn't ignore it he told his hand about it, and later he played the hand back and decided there was definitely something wrong with you because you

61

kept looking at this pointless picture all the time. This behavioural psycho game, easy money or what?

'Now, Jiggy,' he said, removing his hand from his mouth, 'I want you to tell me a bit about yourself. Let's start with school, shall we? What do you think about school?'

I didn't want to think anything about school. School and me didn't see eye to eye right now. Not since Face-Ache Dakin hauled me into the head's office for single-handedly destroying his classroom. Funny, but when it came to it nobody could remember being chased by something noisy, violent and invisible. All they could remember was me tearing a curtain down and going mad, jumping over desks and shouting and stuff. Even when Pete and Angie tried to come to my rescue it didn't do any good. Part of the reason for this was that they couldn't quite bring themselves to say that it wasn't me that had made all the mess in the classroom and terrified the kids, but a dead goose. You can see their point.

Dr Edward Pickett sat there smiling politely while I tried to decide what to tell him about school. The sunshine was sloping through the window really brightly and hitting the picture over his head so hard it glowed.

'What do I think about school...?' I said thoughtfully.

'In your own words,' said Pickett.

I was glad he said that. If he hadn't I might have rushed out into the street and asked a complete stranger what *he* thought of school and rushed right back with the news.

'It's...OK,' I said.

He leaned forward, obviously fascinated by my opinion on this subject. 'OK?'

I shrugged. 'Yeah. OK.'

'You don't mind school?'

I shrugged again. It looked like being a shruggy sort of conversation. 'Sometimes I can think of other places I'd rather be.'

'Such as?'

'Such as the bottom of a coal mine looking for canaries,' I said. 'Such as on the sole of a tramp's shoe when he's just walked in something a horse dropped. Such as at home, in bed.'

'So you don't think much of school?'

'I didn't say that. I said it was OK.'

'So you did.' He spoke briefly to his hand again. 'We might come back to school,' he says then, 'but let's move on now. Tell me about home. Your home life. For instance, how do you get on with your parents?'

I gave shrug three. 'We get on all right.'

'Just all right?'

'What do you want, violins and sunsets? They're my parents.'

'What I want, Jiggy,' Pickett said, like he was trying to talk his cat down from a tree, 'is for you to feel free to talk about them any way you please, in your own words.'

My own words again. I looked at his hair. Then, so as not to seem rude, I looked at the pointless picture above it. The sun coming through the window was getting brighter by the minute and the picture was so dazzling now that the colours looked as if they were moving. I was starting to hallucinate.

'My parents are great. Most of the time.'

I had to feed him that last bit. He needed it, I could tell. He had to have something to latch on to.

'Most of the time? Not...*all* the time then?'

'Do you get on with your parents all the time?' I asked him.

This threw him for a second. 'We're not talking about my parents, Jiggy.'

'Well look at it from my point of view,' I said. 'I mean we're sitting here across from one another, and you, who I never met in my life before, start asking me about my parents. I mean why should I tell you just because my mum brought me here? I'm not being difficult or anything, it's just that I think this should be a two-way sort of thing, that's all.'

He thought about this, then nodded. 'Fair comment. But there's nothing I can tell you, my parents are dead.'

I wished he had a big goldfish bowl so I could stick my head in it and drown. 'Hey,' I said, 'sorry to hear that. I didn't know or I wouldn't have asked. You miss them?'

'Miss them? Well yes. Of course. Sometimes. One does.'

'Does one?' I said.

'Certainly. One's parents, you know.'

'Did you get on with them?'

'We're here to talk about you, Jiggy.'

'All I'm asking is did you get on with your parents, like you're asking me, nothing heavy.'

He gave this some thought too. He was doing his best to be fair. Fair, or maybe he thought he'd get more out of me if he spilled a couple of beans too.

'As a matter of interest,' he said, avoiding my question, 'my mother painted the pictures in this room.'

I looked round the office. 'Yeah? Really?' Now he had me feeling sorry for him. 'Including the one behind you?' The sun was so bright on the big picture now it looked as if it was vibrating. A trick of the light, but it made me nervous.

Pickett glanced up, then back at me. 'That's my favourite.' He must have seen the pity on my face at that because his lips twitched in this way that says I know about these things and you obviously don't. 'I realise they may not be to everyone's taste. Art is such a personal thing.'

'You can say that again.' Fortunately he didn't bother.

'Now tell me about your relationship with your parents,' he said instead, with a very slight shove on the second 'your'.

66

'They'll do,' I said. 'I mean I wouldn't necessarily go to the Parent Shop and pick them out as the pair I most want to spend my childhood with, but they could be worse.'

Pickett flipped his hand to his mouth and while he told it about my parents I watched the sun leak out of the big picture and fan out across the top of his head. It was then that I noticed something. Something so attention-grabbing that I didn't hear a word of what he said to me next. I hadn't been imagining that the picture over his head was moving. It really was, all of it, not just the painting but the frame too. It was coming away from the wall. Falling. In a few seconds it would be off the wall and on Pickett.

And then, about three seconds after I realised the picture was going to squash Pickett, the sun cast a shadow across the painting.

The shadow of a long thin neck with a small beaked head on top.

I jumped up. Ran across the space between the doc and me yelling something like 'Hey, watch out, watch out!'

I reached up, grabbed the picture by the frame,

one hand on each side — but it was too heavy and I was too late! Even with me holding it, it continued on down, and there was this tearing sound, and next thing I knew I was standing there with the frame in my hands looking down at the top of Pickett's head, which was now poking up through the picture. He sat there staring up at me from the back of his dead mother's painting, his favourite pointless picture. The long strands of hair that he'd so carefully oiled on to his dome had come away. They were hanging down past his ear, past his jaw, his neck, the shiny brown ends trailing across the back of the canvas resting on his shoulders. And he looked terrified. Of me.

Then he was getting up out of his chair, shoving it away. Stumbling about all over the place as he tried to wriggle out of the painting, and shouting stuff about me being a delinquent and a vandal, and a hopeless case and a...

Need I go on?

Chapter Ten

The time had come to take my brain out of its box on top of the wardrobe, blow the dust off, and put it to work. I told Pete and Angie to bring their brain boxes too, and together we sat down on the floor in my room to think this thing out.

'Something's got to be done,' I said. 'Something has got to be *done.*'

'Yeah, but what?' said Pete.

'What we need,' said Angie, 'is to be logical about this.'

'Easy to say when you're talking about being haunted by a dead goose,' I chipped in. 'I mean there's logic and logic.'

'And dead geese and dead geese,' said Pete.

'And this,' said Angie, 'is no ordinary dead goose. It's a dead goose that breaks things and chases people and pecks them where it hurts. A poltergoose.'

I nodded. 'That's what we're talking about here, isn't it? A poltergoose.'

'Right,' said Angie.

'Right,' said Pete.

'Question is,' I said, 'what are we gonna do about it?'

'Yeah,' said one of them, or perhaps both. 'That's the question.'

We put our brains back in the boxes. They hadn't worked.

Silence fell. And stayed fallen for some time until Pete suddenly said: 'Ow!' Then he said it again, with echoes – 'Ow-ow-ow-wow-wow-wow!' – and added 'Cramp!' He jumped up, but immediately fell again and lay writhing on the floor, one leg dancing in the air. 'Ow-ow-ow-wow-wow-wow!'

'I get that sometimes,' Angie said. 'Usually first thing in the morning, right after I wake up. It is no fun.'

'I don't think I ever had cramp,' I said.

'You're lucky.'

'Ow-ow-ow-wow-wow-wow!' said Pete.

'I get stitches though.'

'In your side?' Angie said.

'Yeah. And I don't have to be running or anything.'

'Know what you mean. I get them just trying to keep up with my mum in the street. Talk about painful.'

'Ow-ow-ow-wow-wow-wow!'

'And pins and needles,' I said. 'That's almost worse.'

Angie agreed. 'Right. Pins and needles. First time I had them we were visiting this sort of cousin of Mum's, and it was so…*boring* – know what I mean?'

'*Do* I?! Old relatives. The things they talk about to one another. I mean what keeps them *awake*, that's what I want to know.'

'Ow-ow-ow-wow-wow-wow!' said Pete.

'This was one of those really brain-dead Christmas visits,' Angie went on, 'and there's this piano that the sort of cousin is playing songs from 1066 on, and there was nothing else to do but lean on it. The piano.'

'Tough,' I said.

'Owwwwwwwwwwww,' said Pete.

'And I'm leaning there and I get this weird feeling in my elbow that spreads through my whole arm, and I start dancing around yelling "I've broken my arm, I've broken my arm!"', and everybody laughs fit to burst, which didn't help at *all*. I mean *I* didn't know it wasn't fatal, did I? Adults!'

Pete stopped shaking his leg. 'Whew,' he said. 'Next time that happens I'm sawing it off.'

I got up. Walked across the room to put some music on. I was flipping through my tapes and CDs when Angie said: 'Oh very funny, Jig. I'm killing myself here.'

'Whassat?' I said, without turning round. 'I really must get some new stuff. There's nothing here under three weeks old.'

'How do you do that anyway?' Pete asked. 'Clever. Specially as we can't see your hands.'

'My hands?'

'You've been practising, haven't you?'

'What are you on about?' I turned round. 'Practising what?'

They were sitting there on the floor gazing at this stretch of wall that had been blank and would still be blank if it wasn't for the shadow on it. My saliva turned to dust.

'That's nothing to do with me,' I said.

72

Pete and Angie turned to look at me. 'You can't fool us.'

I watched the goose shadow's eye-hole close slowly, then open again. I held my hands out so they could see them. They looked from me back to the wall. The shadow was still there. The beak opened.

'You're...not doing that?' Angie said.

SSSSSSssssssSssssSSSSSsssss

She and Pete got up. Slowly. Backed away from the shadow wall. Slowly. When they reached me we stood as close together as we could without actually climbing into one another's clothes.

'What now?' one of us said.

'Run?' said another.

'Right,' said whoever's turn it was next.

We would have too. Except that as we set off at a fast tiptoe round the edge of the room, each trying to put someone else in front and someone else behind, the goose shadow turned its head to follow us.

But then the sun went behind a cloud and the goose faded to nothing. We gave a big gasp of relief. Three gasps. Angie stepped away from the rest of us to investigate the sudden shortage of goose shadow. And lived to regret it.

'YAAAAAAAAAAAAAAAAAAAAAH!' she said as she flew across the room.

Angie Mint lay in a crumpled heap on the floor just below the wall she'd almost hit. It could have been nasty. She might have gone just that bit further and ruined the wallpaper.

'You all right?' I said from where I was.

'Do you mind if I don't answer that?' the crumpled heap replied.

'Cool with me, Ange,' I said.

Angie came back across the carpet, on her end, a bit at a time like she was half expecting to be picked up and thrown again. When she made it back to us we stood waiting for something else to happen. Nothing did. Even the sun stayed behind its cloud.

'I think we ought to make a move,' Pete whispered.

'I just did and look what happened,' Angie said.

'Well I'm not sticking round here to be thrown at walls.'

'See you then,' I said.

'See you,' Pete replied. He didn't move.

'Well go on if you're going,' Angie said.

'I will, I will. When I'm ready.'

There was a long pause. Pete stayed put.

'When are you going to be ready?' I asked him.

'When I'm *ready* already, all right?'

'Right.'

An even longer pause. Then, very quietly, 'OK,' and he was off, heading for the door. Running.

But what a run. A run like no other I ever saw in real life. Not a fast-as-lightning get-me-outta-here type run. No, this was in slowmotion like in an action film, and there was nothing he could do about it. A Zimmer frame could have passed him.

When Pete was halfway across the room, running for all he was worth at a hundred metres a month, the door opened. By itself. Pete looked happier about that than he did about running slowly. Door open, that meant he could go. He would be out there on the landing any day now.

And he would have been too if not for one small detail. The one small detail was that just as he was about half an arm short of it, the door closed again.

The door closed but still Pete went on. He couldn't stop. He was going so fast now he could almost pass a wounded snail. He reached for the door handle. He turned it. Pulled at it. The door wouldn't budge.

SSSSSSsssssSSssssSSSSSSsssss

Pete yelled, clutched the front of his jeans where he'd just been pecked, and bounced back into the room at suddenly normal speed.

Some minutes later, when we were once again sitting on the floor, backs to the wall, Angie said: 'You know what I think? I think the goose doesn't actually mean us any harm.'

Pete gaped at her in disbelief. 'Doesn't mean us any harm? After what it just did to me?'

'That didn't really hurt. It just gave you a little nip or you wouldn't have any colour in your cheeks.'

'You know,' I said, 'Ange might have something there. The goose could have slammed her against the wall but it dropped her short. And you know in class? It only *scared* the kids, nothing else. And when it pecked me down the stairs it didn't really do any damage, just sort of…rattled me.'

'That's right,' Angie said. 'I think it's simply trying to make us notice it.'

'It succeeded,' said Pete.

HONK!

Our heads hit the wall behind us.

'It's still here,' I said, in case nobody else had realised.

'And honking,' said Angie.

'Old Brooky's goose used to honk like that.'

'All geese do that,' Pete said.

'You don't think it could *be* old Brooky's goose?' This was Angie.

'Nah. Even geese have to be dead before they can haunt people.'

'Has anyone seen Brooky's goose about lately?'

'Well of course we haven't,' I said. 'The farm isn't here any more.'

'Probably lives with him in that new bungalow of his,' said Pete.

HONK!

'I think we'd better go and find out for sure,' said Angie.

HONK! HONK! HONK!

'Definitely,' I said.

We slid up the wall, very, very slowly. There was a low hiss from across the room.

'It's all right, goosey.' Angie waved her hands at nothing in a calming sort of way. 'We're on your side. We're the good guys.'

'We are?' Pete said. 'I thought we were trying to get rid of it.'

HONK! HONK! HONK! HONK! HONK!

We made a run for it. This time the goose didn't do any haunty sort of tricks like make us go in slow-mo, or open and close the door just as we got to it, or throw us across the room. Maybe it knew it had got through to us. Maybe we were on to something here. We threw ourselves down the stairs and out into the street.

Chapter Eleven

The bungalow that Linus Brook had bought with the dosh he got for his cruddy old farm was about where his cow shed used to be. Like my brainless parents, Brooky had given his new home a name. The name he gave his bungalow was painted on a bit of black slate beside the plastic bell push.

LAST STAND

We pressed the plastic bell and waited till the national anthem finished so old Brooky could stop standing to attention on the other side of the glass door and open it.

'Hi, Mr Brook,' I said.

There were huge bags under his eyes and he hadn't shaved for a week. There was no collar on his shirt and not many buttons either. There was dirt beneath his nails, enough hair in his ears to thatch a poodle, and his teeth were yellow, black, or at the dentist's without him.

'Shove off,' he snarled. Same lovable old Brooky.

'It's us,' I said. 'Jiggy, Pete and Angie from Borderline Way.'

'Angie, Pete and Jiggy,' said Angie.

'Pete, Angie and him,' said Pete.

'Never 'eard of you,' said Brooky, and slammed the door.

We looked at one another. Something had gone wrong somewhere. Angie pressed the bell again. Ten minutes later when the national anthem had died once more, Brooky ripped the door back.

'You remember us,' Angie said brightly before he could get a word out. 'We used to help out on the farm in the holidays.'

'For peanuts,' Pete muttered. He never did care for old Brook.

'A lot of kids helped on the farm. If you can call it help. No reason to come bothering me here, I'm retired.'

He slammed the door. We stood looking at it, and at him standing behind the glass like a statue, either waiting for us to go or try again.

'This is ridiculous,' I said.

'Yep,' said Angie.

'Leave it to me,' said Pete, and stepped forward. He didn't bother with the bell. He used his fist.

The door opened.

'I s'pose you think you can get a free cup of tea outta me,' Mr Brook said.

'Only if you're making some,' Angie said over Pete's shoulder.

'Making some what?'

'Er – tea?'

'Why would I make tea?' he growled. 'I hate tea. I always hated tea. Tea is my most hated thing on earth. After kids, that is.'

He slammed the door. Once again we stood looking at it. It was a nice enough door, but not so nice we wanted to spend our lives in front of it.

'Was he always like this?' I said.

'Like what?' said Pete.

I punched him on the shoulder. He punched me back. The door flew open. Old Brook grabbed us by the punched shoulders.

'Oi! I won't have you young layabouts fighting on my doorstep!' And he banged our heads together. 'Now clear orf a'fore I buys a dog and sets it on you.'

While Pete and I staggered about groaning and holding our heads Angie stepped between us and put a foot in the door that old Brooky was about to slam for the fourth time. Being in pain, I wasn't paying much attention but when Ange said the word 'goose' I saw Brooky pass a hand over his eyes and his chest cave in.

'There used to be one round the farmhouse all the time,' Angie was saying. 'Remember her?'

Suddenly, Brooky let out this tremendous wail and fell face down on the Welcome mat, sobbing.

Angie dropped to her knees beside him. 'Mr Brook...?'

Old Brooky twisted his head from the neck to look up at her. His face was all wet.

'What a bird,' he said.

'Hey, that's our mate!' said Pete.

'I think he means the goose,' I said, still reeling a bit.

'Aunt Hetty,' said Brooky, and stuck his nose back in the mat. 'Sob, sob, sob. Sob, sob, sob, sob, sob, sob, sob!'

'Aunt Hetty,' Angie said over the sobs. 'Is that the name of your goose?'

82

'Was,' he said to the mat. 'Wa-a-a-a-a-a-as.'

'Was!' Angie sat back in triumph and beamed up at us. 'So she *is* dead! Good news!'

'EEEERRRRAAAAAGGGHHH!' wailed Linus Brook, miserable old farmer turned miserable old retired bungalow-dweller.

'Why don't we get him off the mat?' I suggested.

The pounding in our heads easing off at last, Pete and I got under Brooky's armpits and hauled him to his feet. Then we half carried, half dragged him into his living room. We were just about to drop him in a chair facing a cold radiator when Angie said: 'Look at this.'

She'd gone on ahead and was standing by the mantelpiece. We joined her, carting Brooky along with us. She was looking at a framed photo of the goose that had been better than a guard dog.

'Hetty.' Brooky reached between us and grabbed the goose photo. A great fat tear squeezed out of his eye, plopped on to the glass. He smeared it away with a thumb.

Then, bit by bit, we got the story. Brooky told us that his wife had never cared for his favourite goose, Aunt Hetty, but when Mrs Brook died he took Hetty in, gave her the guest room. He called it the Guest Goose Room and decorated it specially, goosey wallpaper, goosey curtains, goose feather pillows, the works.

'Real company she was. Someone I could really talk to. Never could talk to the wife. All she ever did was sit there knitting and watching telly. But Hetty, she wasn't keen on the telly. Didn't seem to see any point in it. And as for knitting...'

'What happened to her?' Angie asked, all soft and dewy-eyed.

Brook was now sitting in a chair, the photo of the goose on his lap. 'I killed her,' he said.

Angie's face turned to stone. Her eyes went as hard as boiled sweets. Her voice became a foghorn.

'YOU KILLED HER? YOU KILLED YOUR *FRIEND*?'

Brooky shook so hard his last few teeth almost popped out. He shrank deep into his cardigan.

'I mean in a manner of *speaking*. I didn't *actually* kill her. Not personally. I wouldn't do a thing like that. If she was still alive I'd have her here with me at *Last Stand*. I...I *loved* that goose.'

Angie unclenched her fists and took several

84

deep calming breaths and tried to look sympathetic again. 'So what happened?'

'I'd just sold the land,' Brooky answered, twitching in one damp eye. 'The builders were laying the foundations of the new houses and old Het didn't like all those strangers about the place with their thumping great vehicles, their radios, sandwiches and all. Thought they was trespassing. I had to keep her in when the builders were about.'

'*And?*' Angie said, just managing not to tap her foot.

'Well, my house was the last thing to go. They had to build this place for me before I'd let 'em knock the house down. But one day Hetty got out. I don't know how. I'd gone into town for my pension. When I got back she was lying there, squashed flat. Dead as a doornail. One of the builders had run over her with his bulldozer.'

'Goosedozer,' Pete muttered.

'They said it was an accident,' Mr Brook went on, 'and maybe it was, but I always had this suspicion that she had a go at them and they did her in. Saddest day of my life, that was, seeing poor Hetty lying there like that. No more honking, no

85

more hissing, no more knocking the ornaments over when the national anthem started up.'

I leaned closer to him. I had a personal interest in this. 'What happened to the body, Mr Brook?'

'The body?' He looked up at me and gave another of his pathetic little sobs. 'It was all I could do to dig the grave. All my fault, see. That's what I meant. I as good as killed her when I sold the farm. If I hadn't sold up she'd still be here today, with me.'

'Yes. But where did you bury her?'

'Right where she fell,' he said. 'Right where she fell. I couldn't have carted her off to someplace else, I was too upset.'

'Yeah,' I said, 'but where was *that*?'

'Where?' He gave this some serious thought. 'I don't know,' he said at last. 'One of the new gardens they were laying out, I think.'

'I don't suppose it's any good asking you…which garden?'

He shook his head. 'All looked the same to me. Still do.' He lifted the goose photo and stared at it, the tears welling up again. 'Felt bad about that later on, burying her just anywhere, but it was too

86

late by then, the houses were sold. All private property and none of it mine.' He gave an enormous sigh. 'Should have given old Het a decent burial. The wife had one, and I liked Hetty better.'

When we left Brooky's there was one big question in our minds: if the poltergoose was Aunt Hetty's restless spirit and her body was buried in one of the new gardens and the garden happened to be mine, which *part* of the garden was she in? It would have helped quite a lot if Mr Brook had left a gravestone or something. Mum could always have grown something against it.

'Yeah, but even if we did find Hetty's body,' Pete said as we strolled back to my place, 'it wouldn't mean she's the poltergoose, would it? Necessarily.'

'Bit of a coincidence if she wasn't,' Angie said.

'Maybe. But if we found it and it *was* the poltergoose's...'

'Yes?' I said.

'Well, what would we do with it?'

'We'd move it. Bury it somewhere else. If she's somewhere else she might stop haunting me.'

'Then she might haunt *someone* else.'

87

'Their problem. Me, I'll be out celebrating.'

'Maybe Hetty's haunting you because she *wants* you to move her,' Angie said.

'What, to someone else's garden?'

'No, not someone else's garden. Perhaps she wants a decent burial, like old Brooky's wife.'

'I don't think they hold funeral services for dead geese,' I said.

'I don't mean an actual service. But from what Brooky said he treated her as almost human. So perhaps Aunt Hetty *thought* of herself as human. If she did, naturally she'd want to be laid to rest in a human sort of way.'

'You don't mean in a *coffin*?!' Pete said.

'No, I mean just...just something better than being dropped in a hole near where she hissed her last.'

'Like what?' I said. 'Like where?'

'If I was her,' Angie said, 'I'd want to be put in a place where I'd been happy. Like the farmhouse. I bet she loved it there. Yeah, bury her where the house used to be and her spirit might find peace and stop bugging people.'

'Snag,' Pete said.

'There's always a snag with you, isn't there?' I said to him. 'What now?'

'You know what they built where Brooky's house was?'

'What?'

'The new shopping centre.'

Chapter Twelve

Back home Mum was out in the garden working on her rockery. 'Nice rockery, Peg,' said Pete, the crawler.

Mum looked pleased. 'Well thanks, Pete.'

It really was coming on a treat though. She'd planted half the planet in it by this time and was as proud of it as Dad was of the Rodadoodah bush still being alive.

'Are you going to be out here long?' I asked her.

'Why, do you want company while you mow the grass for me?'

'No chance. Gardening's for wimps. Just asking.'

'As a matter of fact I'm going to the shops in a minute. Is there anything you want – apart from crisps, chocolate, fizzy drinks, and everything else that does you no good at all?'

'No, just those.'

We went up to my room. And –

SSSSSSSsssssssSSsssssSSSSSSsssss

The goose's shadow was waiting for us on the wall. Pete backed into me. 'Let's go,' he said.

'No,' Angie said. 'We have to sort this thing out once and for all. And did you notice anything about that hiss? It was almost gentle. As if it's glad to see us.'

SSSSSSSsssssssSSsssssSSSSSSsssss

She was right. Gentle. Definitely gentle. Angie stepped further into the room.

'Goose,' she said boldly to the shadow on the wall. 'Goose, are you Aunt Hetty?'

And you know what the goose-shadow did? It winked. True as I stand here. Then dipped its neck a couple of times like it was saying 'You got it gal'.

'Yes!' I said, punching air.

'I've got an idea.' Angie held her arm out so the sun cast a shadow of it on the wall, then opened her hand so its shadow was offering a palm to the goose-shadow.

And Aunt Hetty's shadow dipped its beak and touched the shadow of Angie's hand – very gently.

'Hey,' Pete said, impressed.

'You feel anything, Ange?' I said.

'Sort of a tickle. I think she wants to be friends.'

'Ask her if she's buried in my garden.'

'She might not like to think about where she's buried. She might throw me at the ceiling or something.'

'We've got to chance it.'

'You mean I have.' But she squared up to the goose-shadow and cleared her throat. 'Aunt Hetty, are you buried in Jiggy's garden?'

SSSSSSsssssSSsssSSSSSsssss

'Sounds like a yes,' said Pete.

'Ask her if she can show us where exactly,' I said.

'Hetty, can you show us exactly where you're buried?'

The goose-shadow nodded.

'Ask her if she'd like us to dig her up and bury her somewhere else,' I said.

'Would you like us to dig you up and bury you somewhere else?'

SSSSSSsssssSSsssSSSSSsssss

'Ask her if she wants to be buried where

Mr Brook's old house was.'

Angie turned on me. She seemed peeved. 'Why am I doing all the asking? Your mouth seized up all of a sudden?'

'You're doing such a great job,' I told her.

'Huh!' But she asked. 'Hetty, do you want to be buried where the old farmhouse used to be?'

SSSSSSssssssSSsssSSSSSsss

'That is one clever dead goose,' I said admiringly.

'Not necessarily,' said Killjoy Pete. 'Maybe "SSSsssss" is the only word she can say.'

There was a sudden knock on the door. Have you noticed how knocks on the door are always sudden? Not only in books either.

'Can I come in, kids?'

Silent Panic. If Mum came in she'd see the...

We needn't have worried. The shadow of the goose vanished while we blinked.

I opened the door.

'I'm off now. Will you be all right here for half an hour?'

'Sure,' I said. 'Great. Take longer if you want. Take all day. In fact—'

'Thank you, Jiggy, half an hour should do it. I'm just getting a few things in for the house-warming dinner.'

'The what? Oh yeah, that. I thought it was tomorrow.'

'It is tomorrow, but I have some things to prepare and I want it to be really special.'

I glanced at Pete and Angie. They glanced back. All our faces said, Saaaaaaad. House-warming dinner. The things Golden Oldies get up to, breaks your heart.

The poor old parent was about to leave us in peace when she remembered something. 'Jiggy, I've been meaning to ask. Where did you put that sweater your gran sent you?'

'Sweater?'

'The one she went to such trouble to knit for you with her own hands? The one with your *name* on?'

'Oh that thing. I stuck it under the bed.'

'Well would you kindly *unstick* it and put it in your sweater drawer?' She turned away. I started to

94

close the door. 'Oh and Jiggy.'

Angie and Pete and I looked at the ceiling. 'Yes, Mother?'

'Try not to turn the house to rubble while I'm gone – please?'

It wasn't till we heard the front door close that Aunt Hetty's shadow came back. Then I said: 'Ready, Musketeers?'

Pete and Angie nodded. So did Hetty.

'One for all and all for lunch,' three of us said. Hetty just hissed.

We went downstairs. On the way down we could see Hetty's shadow along with ours where patches of sunlight fell on the wall, but once we were out in the garden we couldn't see her at all. It was very bright out there.

'Aunt Hetty?' I said.

SSSSSSssssssSSsssSSSSSsssss

Which as everybody knows is Goose for 'Yep! Here!'

'Show us where you're buried, Het.'

There was a pause. A long pause.

'Perhaps she doesn't know,' said Pete.

'It may not be easy finding your own body,'
I pointed out.

'I never have any trouble,' he said.

HONK! HONK! HONK! HONK! HONK!

'I think she's found herself,' Angie said.

The excited honking had come from the far end of the garden, the out of sight part of the L-shape. We jumped over Mum's terrific new rockery, brushing the flowers and stuff with our heels, and ran round the corner. I was getting this sinking feeling.

'Say again, old goose,' Pete said. 'We're not psychic.'

HONK!

The sinking feeling hit my trainers. My feet twitched. A Latin-American rhythm started to jerk through me. I sniffed one of the perfect little pink flowers, dancing. Here of all places. Aunt Hetty's body was sitting right under the only thing my dad ever planted that lived. His pride and joy. The Rodadoodah bush.

Chapter Thirteen

After we laid the Rodadoodah bush on the grass beside its hole, we dug on with a spade and a couple of trowels from the shed. We all saw it at once. The sack that contained the body. We were pretty pleased with ourselves until we realised that none of us wanted to actually touch it.

'What say we cover it up again?'

'Mm. Good plan.'

'Could do it tomorrow.'

'Or the day after.'

'Even better.'

But like the good brave Musketeers we were we reached in and took hold of the sack, shuddered a bit, and tugged. It didn't want to come up, but we got it out eventually and stood wiping our hands on our jeans in case they'd touched worms or something else too disgusting to think about.

'Go on then,' Pete said. 'Open it.'

'No, you,' I said, breaking into a silent tap-dance on the turf.

'Your garden, your goose.'

'Be my guest.'

'Oh – men!' Angie said, and elbowed us aside.

She untied the sack and spread it open. We looked in. It was not a pretty sight. Even Hetty sounded affected by it.

SSSSSSssssssSSsssssSSSSSSsssss

Then the smell hit us. You could almost see it rising. Three earth-stained hands slapped over three noses, passing the stain on. Angie closed the sack.

'Better put the bush back,' I said, taking the lead in a fox-trot.

It wasn't till the Rodadoodah was back in it's hole that I stopped dancing and just sagged for a while. Without the sack down there below it the bush was about half its former height. A couple of days later I found Dad walking round it, muttering 'I don't get it, I don't get it, I followed all the instructions. I even watered it once.'*

Still, there was nothing we could do about it.

---

* By then it wasn't just a dwarf Rodadoodah, it was a dead dwarf Rodadoodah without a single dinky little pink flower to its name.

'Right,' I said, two days before my father's Great Sorrow. 'The shopping centre.'

Pete pulled a face. 'Are you out of your skull? Where was it your mother just went?'

'Oh yeah,' I said.

'Besides,' said Angie. 'Broad daylight when everything's still open may not be a good idea. And we haven't decided where to rebury her yet.'

'I thought we said where the farmhouse used to be.'

'They built the main square over the farmhouse. We can't dig up the main square, someone might notice.'

'It's not all paved over. What we have to work out is where one of the rooms was, and if it's the sort of spot you can leave dead geese in we're in business.'

'Wait a minute,' Angie said. 'There's this big old tree in the square, with railings round it. Used to be in Brooky's front yard.'

'I don't remember a tree with railings in Brooky's front yard,' Pete said.

'It didn't have railings then, dummy,' said Ange.

'Yeah, that's right,' I said. 'The biggest branch hung right over the house. So all we have to

99

do is see what's under the branch now. Good thinking, Angie.'

'What if it's solid concrete?' Pete said.

'Then we have a problem,' I said.

'Hetty's very quiet,' said Angie.

'Maybe something to do with the fact that she's dead?' said Pete.

'I mean poltergoose Hetty.'

'Probably in shock,' I said. 'Wouldn't you be if you came across your bones and stuff in an old sack?'

'Hetty?' Angie called softly. 'Aunt Hetty, you there?'

Not a sound. Nothing.

'Perhaps she's cleared off now we've found her body,' Pete said. 'Perhaps we can just chuck it over a hedge and go and watch telly.'

SSSSSSssssssSSsssSSSSsssss

'Or maybe not.'

There were several hours to kill before the shopping centre closed, so we had to hide the sack. There was only one place we could think of.

'Look, Hetty,' I said to the empty air, 'don't get

100

your feathers in a twist or anything, we'll take you out later, I promise. It's just to keep you safe, all right?'

The good thing about the wheely bin was that it had been emptied that morning. It still whiffed a bit (though it was pretty sweet after the open sack) but it did the job. It must have been OK with Aunt Hetty anyway, because we didn't hear a peep out of her as we dropped the sack containing her sad old feathers and bones in the bin.

Chapter Fourteen

It was eight o'clock, the time we'd arranged to meet by the wheely bin. Pete and Angie were late. When they finally turned up Angie said it was because Pete kept finding other things he'd rather do than spend the evening with a dead goose. We flipped open the wheely.

'Holy underpants!'

'It's a conspiracy!'

'Unbelie*eeeee*vable!'

Mum must have been saving all the rubbish till the bin had been emptied, because it was now three-quarters full of used tins, sticky wrappers and old curry. All of it on top of the Hetty sack.

'We could always wheel it to the shops,' I suggested.

'People might wonder what three kids are doing pushing a wheely bin around,' Angie said. 'And we'd still have to get the sack out when we got there.'

'I'm not going in there,' Pete said. 'Here *or* at the shops.'

Angie called him a name I'd never heard before and took charge for the second time that day, or maybe the third. I raised an eyebrow at her. She was supposed to be the weaker sex. I'd have to have a word with her about this.

'Jiggy, go and fetch some rubber gloves from the kitchen.'

'Rubber gloves? There's only the washing-up gloves.'

'They'll do.'

'Can't. My mum's wearing them.'

'Terrific. Well I want *something* over my hands.' She mused. 'I know. Hankies.'

'Hankies?' said Pete and I together.

The boss snapped her fingers. 'Come on, come on.'

Pete and I fished out our hankies. Angie curled her lip.

'I'll risk the Black Death. Now tilt the bin. Tilt it over as far as you can.'

We tilted the bin until it was almost flat on the ground and most of the stuff inside had tumbled out. We pulled faces, grunted, said things like 'Eeeeerrrgg,' and then Ange – amazing Ange – reached in bare-handed, grabbed the sack, and pulled.

It didn't budge.

'You too,' she ordered.

'Not me,' Pete said.

She screwed her eyes up at him. 'Sorry? Didn't quite catch that.'

He took a corner of the sack in a finger and thumb. So did I.

'Get a *hold* of it!' Angie said fiercely.

We got a hold of it. A couple of hearty tugs and the sack was out and we sat there covered in bin droppings. Most of the garbage was loose stuff, easily shaken off, but the baked beans and curry and bits of soggy cereal seemed to get into everything, and I don't just mean clothes.

'You stink,' said Pete to me.

'It's my dad's new deodorant, *Wheely Bin For Men.*'

The next problem was getting all the rubbish back, which for some strange reason was even less fun than getting it out. When we'd done that we ran back shuddering to the garden for some clumps of grass to wipe ourselves down. (That's how we came to have green stains all over us as well as the rest.) When we got back to the sack we found two cats sniffing at it with interest.

'Shoo!'

'Scat!'

'Get lost!'

Then, all set, we strolled off in the direction of the shops whistling different tunes, hoping that three kids pulling a sack looked normal. Most people ignored us, but a few grinned in that superior way grown-ups have when they're saying to one another: 'Kids, what will they think of next?'

Hey. If only they knew.

Chapter Fifteen

As expected, the shopping centre was deserted by the time we got there. (It's always deserted from about fifteen minutes after the shops close till about nine when the muggers climb out of bed and the drunks start rolling up to dance with the lampposts.) There wasn't even anyone snoozing in the flowerbeds yet. All just about perfect, in fact, for disposing of dead geese.

Until Pete spotted the downside. 'Major snag,' he said.

I thumped him, naturally, but then I saw what he meant. '*Now* whaddawedo?'

We'd forgotten the new security cameras. We stood in a doorway with our sack of goose watching two of them panning for vandals. We would have watched all four, but a couple of them weren't moving. They'd been vandalised.

'There's the tree with the railings,' Angie said.

'Glad you pointed it out, Ange,' I said. 'Nearly missed it there.'

The big old tree that had once grown wild and free in Mr Brook's front yard now stood imprisoned in a neat little railing in the middle of the square. Everything else around the tree might have changed, but you couldn't mistake the enormous branch that used to hang over the house. It still hung there, over the place we had to put Hetty so she could R.I.P. and stop pestering me.

The Brook Farm Shopping Centre Public Toilets.

'The first person to say anything about feeling a bit flushed,' I said, 'is in big trouble.'

'Come on,' Angie said. 'Let's case the joint.'

'Hold on,' Pete said. 'One of the cameras is turning this way.'

We waited while the camera panned slowly by, then made a run for the toilets.

We waited while the camera panned the other way.

Then we ran back for the sack.

'Whew,' said Pete when we were at the toilets again.

I couldn't have expressed it better myself. This

was nerve-wracking stuff. My feet had started moving in small rhythmic circles, my hips were swaying, fingers clicking.

There were two doors to the block of toilets beneath the branch. One of them had the word Ladies over it. The other had the word Gets, because someone had stolen the 'n'. The Gets was boarded up, probably because the graffiti–covered door on the other side of the boards hung on only one hinge.

'This one's OK,' Angie whispered from the next doorway.

We joined her, dragging the sack between us. There were no boards over the other door, it hung on both hinges at once, and it hadn't been locked up for the day yet. Angie went in. The door closed behind her.

Pete and I looked at one another. Then we looked at the door. Then we looked at one another again. Then we looked at Angie, who'd just opened the door to look out at us.

'What are you waiting for, a personal invitation?'

'We can't go in there,' Pete said.

'It's only a toilet,' said Ange.

'It's a *Ladies* toilet,' I reminded her.

'So?'

'Well we're not ladies.'

'Camera's coming,' Pete said.

We pushed past Angie. The door closed behind us. Pete Garrett and Jiggy McCue were in the Brook Farm Shopping Centre Ladies Toilet.

'I'll never live this down,' said Pete.

'Nor will I,' I said.

'I won't tell if you don't,' he said.

'Deal,' I said. We shook hands, then wiped them on our jeans.

Then it hit us. And we thought dead goose in an old sack was bad?

'Phwah!' Pete said, palming his nose into his skull.

I agreed. 'No wonder there's a hole in the ozone layer.'

'Remind me to inspect the Gets sometime,' Angie muttered.

Pete and I looked around. We didn't like to, but it went with the job. What we saw on the walls shocked us to the core.

'I didn't know you got stuff like this in the Ladies,' Pete marvelled. 'I thought it was only fellas wrote this sort of thing.'

'The drawings aren't bad,' I said.

'When you two have stopped admiring the artwork,' Angie said, 'we have to decide where to put Hetty's bones.'

'No problem,' Pete said.

He kicked open one of the three cubicles and bowed like a magician expecting applause. He didn't get it.

'No,' I said. 'Not there. It'd be…disrespectful.'

'She's a goose. She'll probably think it's an honour to be flushed into the main drainage system.'

'You there, Hetty?' I said through the filthy hanky over my face. 'How would you feel about floating out to sea, Het? You wouldn't be alone.'

If she was in there with us she was too choked with emotion to reply. Either that or she'd stayed outside because she couldn't stand the smell.

'Anyway, we'd have to take her apart bone by bone to get her down there,' said Ange. 'And her beak would probably get stuck round the bend. No, we'll have to think of something else.'

'This is a public toilet,' Pete said. 'Public toilets have two things. They have wash-basins and they

110

have…toilets. Got it, or am I going too fast? If you want to get rid of anything here that is the choice. Plug hole or bog. Do you want to take a vote on it?'

'There might be one other place,' I said, strolling over to the basins. There were three of them to match the cubicles. Below the middle one was the drain that all the gungy washing water slopped into. There was an iron grill over the drain. The grill had this nice flowery pattern riddled with holes. I tapped it with my foot.

'It's not much bigger than the toilet,' Pete said.

'Big enough though,' I said. 'Wouldn't have to pull her apart to get her down there, just get her to breathe in a bit.'

'See if you can get the cover off,' Angie said.

My eyes raced over the floor I'd have to kneel on to do that small thing. It wasn't all that clean but for the first time I was glad this was the Ladies rather than the Gets. In the Gets, the customers take aim at the wall, close their eyes, and spray everything they can't see, including their feet, neighbouring trousers, and the ceiling. After a day's zipper action in the Gets, the floor is a swamp. At least this one was dry. I got down on it and inspected the drain cover.

'Anybody got a screwdriver?'

'Sure,' Pete said. 'I always carry a screwdriver. Would you like my hammer and nails while you're at it? My electric sander? My Black and Decker drill?'

Angie leaned down. 'What do you want a screwdriver for? No screws.'

'No, but I have to get something under the grill to pull it up, and a screwdriver would probably do it.'

'Use your fingers.'

'Use *your* fingers,' I said. 'Mine are reserved for earwax duty.'

'Wimp,' she said, and yanked me away from the drain.

She dropped to her knees and hooked her fingers into the grill. I watched, filled with admiration and disgust.

Pete wandered over to the door for a lung of fresh air. Angie and I were still crouched over the drain when I heard him say: 'What do you call a man in an envelope?'

'What are you talking about?' I said.

'It's a joke. What do you call a man in an envelope?'

'I don't know. Don't care.'

'Bill,' he said. No one laughed. Then he said: 'Someone's coming.'

'Is this another joke?'

'No. Someone's coming.'

'Well who?'

'How would I know, she's not carrying a board with her name on it. But she looks like she's coming here – two guesses what for.'

There was a clang followed by a yelp as Angie jumped up and banged her head on the basin. She bolted past me into one of the cubicles and slammed the door. Pete bolted past me into another cubicle and slammed the door. I bolted past me into the third cubicle and slammed the door. I would have bolted the door too, but the bolt was on someone's gate a mile away. I parked my jeans on the seat and slapped my soles against the door.

'Who's got the sack?' Angie's voice, muffled by distance and cubicle walls.

'Not me,' said Pete, also muffled but not quite as much.

'It's still out there,' I informed them.

There was a small pause. We could hear footsteps

now, tappy-tap-tapping in the square.

'Maybe she'll miss it,' said Angie.

'Maybe she won't,' said Pete.

Another small pause. The tappy-taps were closing in.

Angie said: 'Something just occurred to me. There are three cubicles, and they're all full, two of them with boys.'

'Well?' I said.

'Well if that woman wants to use one she's going to be disappointed.'

'Good,' Pete said, 'then she'll shove off.'

'No, she won't. No one would use this place unless they were desperate. She'll cross her legs and wait for an empty cubicle.'

'She'll have a long wait.'

'We can't stay in here for ever.'

'Oh I don't know,' said Pete.

'Pete,' I said. 'Move over, I'm coming in.'

I separated my feet from the door, intending to make a fast switch to his cubicle and jostle for seat space, but just as I opened up the lady punter came in. I froze.

'Hi. Nice evening.'

She also froze. 'This is the Ladies,' she said.

'I know,' I said. 'I was just looking for my sack. Ah, there it is.'

I grabbed the Hetty sack, dragged it past her, smiling hard.

Chapter Sixteen

Out in the square I hid behind the tree in the railings to fool the cameras. The seconds ticked by. I counted them into minutes. One minute, two minutes, three minutes, four. At the stroke of five and a quarter the woman came out and waltzed off round the corner of the supermarket. I lugged Hetty back into the Ladies.

'It's all right, she's gone,' I said to the two closed cubicles.

'Whew!' said Angie.

Her door opened. So did Pete's. He peered out. All the colour had drained from his face. 'That was the most horrible experience of my life,' he said.

'I need help,' said Angie holding her hand up. It was wearing the drain cover. Her fingers were like knitting.

'Leave it to me, Ange,' I said, and bent her fingers back.

She screamed.

I bent them the other way.

She screamed again, but the cover was off.

We set to work.

It wasn't much easier forcing the sack of Hetty remains down that little drain than it had been getting it up out of the Rodadoodah hole, but we did it. That is, Angie did it, with me pushing at her shoulders and her telling me to stop. Pete watched the door. Every now and then he watched the square outside too. No one else came.

I felt quite sad when Hetty and her sack were squashed tight into the drain and Angie had banged the grill back into place. I mean we'd been close in our way. I still had the dents to prove it. But we'd done it. Laid her to rest in the drain of her dreams. And I was a free man again.

When we left the shopping centre I crossed the road to the sparkling new houses of the Brook Farm Estate, and Pete and Angie shunted off towards the Old Town and Borderline Way where half the street lights had been successfully used for target practice and cars lived on bricks.

'Thanks, gang,' I called merrily as we waved goodbye.

'It was a real pleasure,' Pete replied. 'Next time use a neighbour.'

Before I slipped out of the house earlier without telling Mum and Dad, I thought of leaving a compilation CD playing in my room, set on 'Repeat' so it would never finish and they'd think I was still up there. I didn't in the end because I decided that no one would be stupid enough to fall for that one. So the house was silent apart from the TV in the living room as I tiptoed upstairs and opened the door of my room.

Mum and Dad were sitting on the bed, waiting for me. My hand trembled on the doorknob. They looked a little tense.

'We were just going to call the police,' Dad said.

'The police?' I said, my recent life somersaulting past my eyes.

'Where have you been?' said Mum.

'To the toilet. I went to the toilet.'

'No you haven't. We looked in both toilets.'

'Hey,' I said, 'isn't it cool to be able to say that? Couldn't have said that in the old days, at good old Borderline Way.'

'I said where have you *been*, Jiggy?' Mum

repeated, a little coldly I thought.

'Why? Don't tell me I missed something.'

Dad chipped in. 'Cut the smart talk, Jig. Your mum's been worried half out of her tree. And before you go to the trouble of inventing something else I phoned Oliver to see if you'd sneaked off somewhere with Angie and Pete.'

'What did he say?'

'He said you hadn't, they've been upstairs all evening playing the same boring record over and over.'

'Enough of this,' Mum said. She leaned forward, gritted her teeth, spoke in italics. *'Where – have – you – been?'*

I thought furiously. 'I went for a walk,' I said. 'Round the estate. To see how the gardens are coming along, count the gnomes – you know.'

'Jiggy, I've told you before, I do not want you wandering the streets at night. The sort of people that hang round out there, it's simply not safe.'

'You've got to let me out sometime,' I said.

'Yes, well let's wait till you stop reading comics, shall we?'

'I still read comics,' Dad said.

Mum ground her teeth. 'Mel, that sort of remark doesn't help at all. Look at him, he's relaxed again.'

'Sorry. Not much good at the heavy parent stuff.'

He got up to leave. He was about to pass me when his nostrils shot out like a mad horse's.

'Ever heard of baths, Jig? Or showers?'

I put my fingers to my chin. 'Hmm, that's a tough one.'

'And the state of you, what have you been *doing*?'

'I went out like this.'

'You deal with him,' he said to Mum, and left the room.

When he'd gone Mum said 'Jiggy' in a much gentler voice and reached a hand out for me.

I took it, wondering if I should tell her to get a typhoid jab from the doc afterwards.

'Yes, Mum?'

She pulled me closer. Her nostrils flared too but she was too much of a gentleman to shudder. She sat me down beside her.

'Jiggy,' she said again.

'Still here,' I said.

'Promise me you won't do anything like that again.'

'What, go out? You mean not even to school?

Can I have that in writing?'

'You know what I'm talking about.' Her eyes went all big and soft, and she added: 'You're all we've got, you know.'

'Well that's not quite true,' I said. 'You've got the car, the TV, the washing machine, your curling tongs. And don't forget Stallone.'

She threw my hand away, probably realising it was contaminated, and stood up. She seemed upset about something.

'There's no point in even *trying* to talk to you, is there? Well pay attention to this. I want you out of those things right this minute, you hear me? You will then go and have a good wash – and I mean *good* wash – and go straight to bed. I don't want to see hide nor hair of you till tomorrow morning, when I expect a full apology for worrying me sick. Do I make myself clear?'

'Yes, Mum,' I said.

She went. I leaned back on the bed. Suddenly I felt tired. Very, very tired. All I wanted was to get in there under the duvet and not wake up till the end of the week when school was over. Still, I had the satisfaction of knowing that my poltergoose troubles were over. Never again would I see Aunt Hetty's shadow on my wall. Never again see rocking-horses butchered before my eyes or gorillas fall off hooks or lights torn from ceilings. Never again would I be chased downstairs by a beak.

There was probably a happy grin on my face as my bed suddenly tipped up, flew across the room, and hit the opposite wall with me still on it. As the bed rocked back on its castors and I rolled on to the floor with a bowl of white plastic flowers in my hands, an insane honking, like no honking I ever heard before, filled the room.

But that wasn't all. Not quite. Suddenly these colossal great lumps of soft stuff were hailing down from the ceiling.

Goose droppings from hell.

And then my mother and father were rushing back in screaming my name and threatening to ground me for the rest of my life if I didn't stop this outrageous, this childish, this totally unacceptable behaviour. We didn't discuss the goose droppings. I don't think they wanted to know somehow.

122

Chapter Seventeen

So Hetty didn't care for life after death in a public drain and she wasn't going to leave me in peace till we found her some place more to her liking.

'Pity she didn't mention it before,' Angie said when I told her and Pete at school next day.

'And where else are we supposed to put her?' Pete said.

'I don't know, but it has to be soon, like tonight. At breakfast my dad was looking through *Yellow Pages* for strait-jacket suppliers.'

'We can't do anything tonight. Your parents' wacky house-warming dinner thing.'

'If we don't do it tonight,' I said, 'Hetty might lose her goosey cool and completely destroy the wacky house-warming dinner thing, along with what's left of my sanity.'

'Jiggy's right,' said Angie. 'We have to act fast.'

We arranged to meet by the shopping centre at eight to haul Hetty out of the Ladies and back to my place. Thought we might stick her under the dwarf Rodadoodah again till we figured out what to do next. But then, just before tea, Angie phoned and told me to bring a spade.

'What do we want a spade for?' I asked. 'We can pull her out.'

'It's for putting her where she ought to be.'

'We don't know where she ought to be.'

'I do,' she said. 'I went back to the shopping centre after school and realised where we went wrong. Tell you later. Eight o'clock, with spade.'

At ten to eight, all dressed up in the clothes my mother laid out specially to make me feel really stupid (creases down the front of my jeans and all) I stuck my head round the kitchen door. Mum was bending over the stove like a witch, stirring something, and Dad was sitting on a stool looking at the pictures in the free local paper he never reads.

'Mum, what time's this dinner thing?'

'I told Aud and Oliver eight for eight-thirty.'

'What does that mean?'

'Means we sit down to eat on the dot of 9.43,' Dad muttered from behind the paper.

'So I've got…how long exactly?'

'One hour,' said Mum.

'And a half,' said Dad. 'At least.'

'Where do you think you're going anyway?' Mum asked, looking up from her stirring.

'Meeting Pete and Angie. We'll have a little chat, then they'll come back with me.'

'Then you can go upstairs and put a jumper on. I don't want you getting that clean shirt dirty.'

'I won't get it dirty.'

'Don't argue or I'll remember what I said last night about you not going out again as long as you live.'

I tore all my hair out, jumped on it, and ran back up to my room. I grabbed the first woolly thing in my drawer, stuck my head through it, and hopped down again six stairs at a time.

Out in the garden I whipped a spade from the shed.

'You there, Hetty?' I said.

SSSSSSss

'Come on then, race you! And no beaking!'

I legged it for the shopping centre accompanied

125

by the occasional feathery flap. Like last time, the square was deserted and quiet. Angie and Pete were already there, standing well back from the cameras. Like me, they were in their best togs. They too had embarrassing creases down their jeans.

The first thing Angie said when I jogged into view wasn't, as you might expect, 'Hi, Jig, glad you could make it, see you got the spade, you're my hero.' No, it was: 'Jiggy McCue, are you out of your pathetic excuse for a *mind*?'

'Naturally, only place to be,' I zapped back. 'Why do you ask?'

'The sweater?' she said wearily.

I looked down at my sweater from on high. It was the one my gran had knitted with her own wrinkly little hands. The blue one with JIGGY screaming across the front in luminous orange letters as big as an elephant's behind. My mother had asked me to remove it from under my bed and when I didn't she must have rescued it and put it where I couldn't miss it – where I *hadn't* missed it.

I heard a small gasping sound near my feet. Pete's knees had given way and he was folded up on the ground in silent hysterics. Angie and I stood looking at the sky while he gagged down there for another minute, then he got up, tears streaming down his neck. He couldn't look at me.

The Ladies toilet sat across the square, waiting for us. 'Anyone in there?' I said.

'Not unless they've got a problem,' Angie said. 'We've been here ten minutes. Come on, and mind those cameras – specially you, you berk.'

We loaded our feet and fired them across the square. It wasn't till we reached the Ladies and were halfway through the door that we noticed dirty water splashing up our nice clean jeans. This took our attention away from the smell of the place, but we may have forgotten to be grateful as we slithered to a halt at the wash-basins. From the look of it, the water was bubbling out of the drain underneath instead of gurgling gently into it.

'Must be blocked up with something,' Pete said, wading right back to the door.

'I'm not putting my hand down there this time,' Angie said.

'Come on, Ange,' I said. 'You're so good at it.'

'Well it's about time someone *else* got good at it then, isn't it? Like you.'

'But I'll get all wet,' I said. 'Wetter.'

'That's your brain leaking all over that stupid sweater. Get down there.'

She was in that dangerous mood again. I rolled up my woolly hand-knitted sleeves, plunged a neatly creased knee into the canal that swirled about us, and closed my eyes in misery.

'What's it feel like?' Pete said, leaning in the door on his toes.

'Shut up,' I said.

The drain cover was all slimy, like seaweed or poached slugs. My stomach turned over as I stuck my fingers in. I tugged. The grill didn't budge. I tugged again. Slight movement. I put everything I had into it – and shot backwards, full length, into the water, fingers neatly interwoven with the pretty iron pattern.

'You wanna be careful,' Pete said from the door. 'Spoil your nice party clothes.'

'Angie,' I said, splashing to my feet, 'untie my fingers, will you? I want to put them in Pete's eyes.'

'Get away from me,' she said. 'I'm as wet I'm going to get.'

'*You're* wet?' I said. 'Compared to me you're the Sahara Desert!'

'Do you know what "sahara" means in Arabic?' Pete said. 'Desert. It means desert. True. Read it on a packet of tea the other day. So when we say "Sahara Desert" what we're really saying is "Desert Desert". How about that?'

'I'm gonna kill him,' I said to Angie.

Angie pulled herself together and unlaced my fingers. I dropped the grill into the water. It sank without trace.

'Now the sack,' she said. 'Pete, get in here.'

'No chance,' said Pete.

'PETE!'

He splashed in, scowling. 'This is all your fault, McCue. You and that stupid goose of yours.'

SSSSSSssssssSSsssSSSSsssss

'You still here?' he said.

I stood back while Angie guided Pete's hands into the drain and he grabbed the sack, whimpering.

129

'Well don't just kneel there,' she said to him. 'Pull it out.'

'What do you think I'm trying to do, pluck its feathers one by one?'

But he pulled a bit harder, and pulled again, and once more, and then –

SPLASH!

Over he went, on his back, the sack on top of him. 'Well done, Pete.' I grabbed the sack before it floated away. Pete just lay there, spluttering and thrashing about.

Angie and I went to the door. 'People,' she said, looking out.

There were two of them, a couple, plus a silly little dog, wasting their lives looking in a closed shop window. In a minute they mooched off, but not before the dog had cocked his leg at the window to show what he thought of the display.

'To the tree!' Angie said when their heels had clicked away to nothing.

Dodging the two roving lenses, we dragged the sack across the square, leaving a wet sacky trail for Pete to follow when he stopped doing the back-stroke in the Ladies.

'Hetty?' I said when we got to the tree. 'Are you with us or back there having a paddle with Pete?'

SSSSssss

'Sounds a bit beaked off,' said Angie.

'She's not the only one. So where did we go wrong yesterday?'

'We were facing the wrong way.'

'No, no, can't have been,' I said. 'That branch definitely hung over the house, I remember it vividly.'

'You vividly remember the wrong branch. The one hanging over the toilets is not the one that hung over the farmhouse. Looks the same 'cos it's about the same size, same model, but it's not the one. They lopped off the branch we were looking for when they built the square round the tree to show how much they care about nature.'

'How do you know which one got lopped?'

'Remember the last time we worked for old Brooky, when we went up to the house to plead for our wages? His goose – Hetty, as we now know – came at us like we were Jehovah's Witnesses or something. Half terrified us.'

'More than half,' I said.

'And when she flew at us I fell over this great root.'

'What great root?'

'This great root.'

We looked at the great root at the base of the tree. Most of it was inside the railings but there was a little warning sign near the bit they couldn't get in. The little warning sign said: MIND THE ROOT.

'And this root,' Angie said, 'pointed to the very room where Mr Brook and Hetty played Scrabble in their bedsocks on chilly nights.'

'And now it's pointing at a flowerbed. Which is why you wanted me to bring the spade.'

'Right. But it's a bit exposed, so we'll have to watch those cameras. Dash out, dig, dash for cover when a camera comes, dash out, dig, dash for cover when a cam—'

'What's Pete up to?' I said.

Pete had finally quit the Ladies and was sauntering across the square like a tourist whose luggage has gone to the Bahamas without him. Wet footprints followed him. The cameras took it in turns to sweep across him. We shouted at him to cover his face, and get a move on before he was broadcast to the entire world by satellite.

'I'm past caring!' he shouted back.

Angie had already told Pete her idea so it didn't need to be repeated when he eventually joined us in hiding.

'But we don't know for certain that Hetty wants to be buried in a flowerbed,' I said. 'I mean she hasn't actually *said*, has she.'

'So ask her,' said Ange.

'Hetty,' I said to a nearby patch of empty air, 'now I want you to think carefully before you answer, because I don't want you wrecking my reputation at *The Dorks* again. Or my room. See that flowerbed over there? That's where your old living room was. Now what I want you to tell us is: do you...want us...to bury...your remains...*there*?'

SSSSsssss

'Is that a yes or a no?' Angie whispered.

'Was that a yes or a no, Hetty?'

SSSSSSsssss

'Any questions?' I said to the others.

There were no questions, even from Pete, but that could be because he was too depressed to speak.

Chapter Eighteen

After making sure that the entire local constabulary hadn't suddenly ridden their bikes into the square to take notes (and that the cameras were looking the other way) Angie and I rushed to the flowerbed. As I had the spade it was me who took first dig.

'Camera's coming,' Angie said after two strokes.

We trotted back to the tree, where we'd left the sack with Pete who seemed quite happy to spend his life there, dripping.

'Come on, Pete,' I said. 'One for all and all for lunch?'

'I'm not happy,' he said. 'I'm wet and I'm uncomfortable and the creases have fallen out of my jeans.'

'You *like* creases in your jeans?'

'Doesn't everyone?'

'Camera's gone,' said Ange.

I dashed out again, with her riding my heels.

'Pete!' I hissed.

He drifted after us and stood wringing his pockets out and mumbling.

'Whew,' I said. 'Hot work.'

'You've dug six centimetres,' said Ange.

'Ground's hard.'

'Pete, you take a turn.'

Pete took the spade and turned it over a couple of times as if he'd never seen one before.

'Camera's coming,' I said.

Pete threw the spade in the air and ran for cover like a madman. We followed, not quite as frantically. Those cameras are not fast swivellers.

'I have an idea,' Angie said under the tree.

Pete groaned. 'Just what we need, another idea.'

'It's this. You don't dig, Pete, you just stand here and tell us what the cameras are doing.'

'I like it,' said Pete, cheering up immediately. 'Camera's gone.'

Angie and I dashed out. I started digging again. She snatched the spade from me – 'Give me that!' – and did practically the whole job herself between runs. She didn't hang about either, just got on with it, no hassle, no complaints, no sweat, even under

135

the arms so far as I could tell. Angie Mint, a girl! What a waste.

When the hole was big enough we dropped the sack in and covered it over in double-quick time.

'What about flowers?' Angie said. 'She ought to have flowers.'

'She's got flowers,' said Pete, who was getting it together again at last and running out and back with us. 'She's in a bed of them.'

'Yeah, but look at the state of it.'

We looked at the state of the flowerbed. It wasn't as colourful as it should have been, being as there weren't many flowers in it. We took in the other flowerbeds round the square. Ditto. It was flower pinching season and they were all a little low on stock.

'Let's gather some up,' Angie said.

We raided the other flowerbeds and replanted a fair selection over Hetty's grave between camera swivels.

'Snag,' said Pete, right back on form now.

'Must you keep *saying* that?' I growled.

'Yes, but look. There are so many flowers over Hetty now, and so few everywhere else, that someone's bound to want to know what's down there.'

I hated to admit it, but he was right. So we took a lot of the flowers out again and – dodging the cameras – re-replanted them all over the place so no one would get suspicious.

When we'd finished, I said: 'Shouldn't we say something?'

'How about "Let's get outta here"?' said Pete.

'No, I mean some sort of…prayer or something.'

'I've been saying prayers ever since we arrived.'

'For Aunt Hetty.'

'A prayer for a goose?' he said. 'Gimme a break.'

'Well not a prayer exactly, just a few words. As a way of saying goodbye.'

'I think "Goodbye Hetty" says it all.'

'No, Jiggy has a point,' said Angie. 'This is a big moment in her life after all.'

'In her *life*?' said Pete.

'Camera coming,' I said.

We ran for cover. While we waited for the camera to move off I asked if anyone had anything to write with.

'I've got a felt-tip,' Angie said.

'Painful,' said Pete.

I took the felt-tip. 'Any paper?'

'Not this side of the Ladies,' said Ange.

'Camera's going,' said Pete.

'Hang on, I'm going to write something for Hetty. Turn round, Pete.'

'What for?'

'Just do it.' I spread my snot-stiffened hanky across his back and started to write. I didn't let them see till I'd finished.

'That's not right,' Pete said then.

'I know it's not *right*, I've adapted it for the occasion.'

'It doesn't *fit* the occasion.'

'Well it's short notice, you got any better ideas?'

He hadn't. Nor had Angie. 'It'll have to do,' she said. 'Hang around here much longer and we'll be released on video, with a commentary and theme tune.'

We went back to the flowerbed, where we gathered in a solemn row of three and I held up my hanky and we read my immortal lines, which I'd done a fair job of arranging round the hard little black bits, I thought.

138

'Hey diddle-diddle
The cat did a piddle
A cow pat fell off the moon
The little dog barked to see such fun
And the goose flew away too soon.'

And then the most amazing thing happened. Just as we finished my farewell to Aunt Hetty there was this incredible noise from overhead. Naturally we looked up. And saw a flock of geese flying across the sky in this great V-shape.

'Now that,' Pete said, 'is what I call a coincidence.'

As they flew the geese flapped their wings so slowly you wondered how they stayed up there. Their necks were stretched right out, and their beaks made this sound, like a cross between a pack of hounds chasing a fox and a bunch of cracked old bells. I think I said 'Wow'.

'Twenty-four,' Angie breathed in my ear.

'Uh?'

'There's twenty-four of them. Eleven on one side, twelve on the other, plus the one in front making the point of the V. Twenty-four.'

HONK!

We grabbed hold of one another. That was one loud honk. And close. 'Hetty...' one of us said, or perhaps it was all of us.

HONK!

Not quite so loud this time, and up a bit. Then there it was again.

HONK!

And again, and again, and again. And each time invisible Hetty honked she did it a bit further away, a bit higher up the sky.

HONK!

HONK!

HONK!

HONK!

'Awesome...' Pete murmured.

The shadow of a flying goose had appeared, very high up, approaching the V-shaped formation.

'Go on, girl,' I said. 'Go on, you can do it.'

'Twenty-five!' Angie laughed as Hetty clicked into place at the tail-end of the shorter line.

'Awesome,' said Pete again.

'Awesome,' said Angie.

'Awesome,' said I, and hoisted the spade to wave goodbye to the dear old goose.

140

Chapter Nineteen

As we approached the back gate we heard music. Well, music. Sad Golden Oldie stuff so ancient that N̆ah danced to it with a hippo in the Ark. We opened the gate. I hid the spade. We went round the 'L'. Audrey Mint and Oliver Garrett and Dad were on the patio admiring Mum's rockery. Dad obviously hadn't been to look at the Rodadoodah lately because he was smiling. All three of them were in their best clothes and all clean and shiny. Unlike us. They noticed this. So did Mum when she trotted out of the house five seconds later.

'Jiggy! I don't believe what I'm seeing!'

I held my hands up. I'd had it with explanations.

'Well whatever you've been up to you can just go right upstairs this minute and wash. All of you. And you,' she said, glaring at me in particular, 'can change out of those *filthy* things.'

'I'll lose the sweater,' I said.

'You'll lose the lot. Your other jeans are in your wardrobe.'

'I can't change my jeans. Then I'll be the only neat one.'

'He has a point, Peg,' said Audrey. 'Unless you think we should take the other two home to change too…?'

Mum threw her bottom lip out. 'The meal's about ready.'

'Oh, leave 'em be,' my dad said. 'They've looked worse.'

Mum threw some daggers at him but he ducked and she gave in.

'Very well, but give yourselves a *good* wash. And be sharp about it, we're eating in five minutes!'

We went upstairs. I ran along the landing and threw my bedroom door back. 'Hetty?'

No answer. And the room felt different somehow. Gooseless. I could live with that.

'Gone!'

'And good riddance,' Pete said. 'I never *ever* want to see another goose, alive or dead.'

'Nor me,' said Ange.

We went to the bathroom. I looked at the taps

over the sink, decided it would be a shame to make the handles dirty, and went back to my room where I finally found a use for Roger the gorilla, brushing off earth and other gunge with his stupid arms. I was just dumping Gran's sweater back under the bed when Mum called.

We went down, past the kitchen where the old dear was slaving away on her own. 'Smells great, Mum,' I said to cheer her up. 'Hope it's chips.'

'It's not,' she said, miserable as sin.

We went out to the garden.

'You look very pleased with yourselves,' Oliver said.

'That's 'cos we're young and have our whole lives ahead of us,' Pete said, 'and you're old and you've had yours.'

Oliver gave him a nasty grin. 'Cheeky little B.'

'Have you heard the news?' my dad said to us.

'What news?'

He glanced at Audrey and Oliver. 'Can I tell them or do you want to?'

Oliver put his arm round Aud, still grinning. 'Go ahead, Mel.'

Pete clutched his head. 'Oh no, they're gonna get *married*.'

A strangled sound came from Angie. 'They can't do that. Then you and I would be related. Almost...brother and sister.'

A dozen freckles jumped off Pete's nose in alarm. 'You can't be best mates with your sister, it's impossible!'

Dad and Aud and Oliver had picked up on some of this and were chuckling like billy-o.

'No, no, no,' Oliver said. 'We wouldn't be daft enough to get *married*.'

Aud's grin twitched almost to nothing. She lurched away from him. 'No, we'd never do something as daft as *that*.'

'Whew,' said Pete and Angie together and slapped palms.

'They're going to buy a house on the estate,' Dad said. 'We're all going to be neighbours again!'

More freckles popped off Pete's nose. 'You mean move? Move from Borderline Way?'

'Don't worry, Pete,' Mum said as she came out from the kitchen again, 'we know a good behavioural psychologist who no longer has a picture over his chair. It's ready, everyone.'

The Golden Oldies rubbed their hands together

and stampeded into the house.

'It's not *so* bad on the estate,' I said as we trailed after them. 'Once you get used to the newness and all.'

'Yeah, but I've lived on Borderline Way all my life,' Pete said.

'So had I, but I made it out of there and survived – just.'

'And we'll all be able to go to school together again,' Angie said.

Pete grunted. 'Better than getting related to one another, I s'pose.'

'Million times better than *that*,' said Ange.

We went into the house. The dining room looked a treat. Mum had really done a job there. Napkins in wooden rings and bright new cutlery and table-mats and dishes of veg and sauces and stuff. No chips. Dad was already in his place at one end of the table and Audrey and Oliver sat on one side, with the three chairs opposite them meant for us. There was a bit of a scuffle while we jostled one another for the best seats. Angie got the middle one and smacked our arms till we stopped trying to get her out of it.

'All set, everyone?' Mum bawled from the kitchen.

'All set!' we all bawled back.

She came in carrying this huge silver platter that I hadn't seen before, with this huge silver dome on it.

'What is it, Mum? Chicken?'

'Wait and see.'

'Turkey? Can't be turkey, it's summer.'

She set the silver platter down in the space she'd left for it in the middle of the table.

'Hope you all like this. Otherwise it's back to the tin opener.'

Six heads leaned forward, twelve nostrils twitching in anticipation as Mum lifted the silver dome. And there it was, our house-warming dinner. Big, plump, steaming, and so tender-looking you could almost taste it already. Three grown-ups slapped their lips and reached for their forks so they wouldn't have to waste any time when it was on their plates.

'Mum,' I said nervously. 'Mum, it's not…it's not a…?'

'It's a goose, darling,' Mum said. 'I don't think you've ever had roast goose befo— Jiggy?'

My chair hit the wall behind me as I jumped up. *Splat*.

'What's up with you?' Dad said in surprise.

Two more chairs hit the wall. *Splat*. *Splat*. Pete and Angie were also on their feet.

'Angie!'

'Pete, what the hell are you playing at?'

Hands over our mouths, skin the colour of old broccoli, we broke all records for table-to-door sprinting, hoofed it along the hall, past the kitchen, out the back door. We made it to the garden only just in time, where we threw ourselves gratefully on to my mother's terrific new rockery.

'One for all and all for luuuuuunnnn...'

We almost got it out, almost but not quite. Got something else out instead. Mum didn't appreciate that. Nor did the others. You know the way parents stick together at times like that, gang up on you because they're bigger and fatter and pay the pocket money. Mum said she'd never be able to look at that rockery again without seeing the three of us sprawled across it heaving into it like there was no tomorrow. I felt the same, but for me it was one of those great moments. The Three Musketeers, side by side, us against the world. Pals, mates, chums. Buds to the bitter end.

Chapter Twenty

Guess what. The local paper just came through the door, and right there on the front page there's a picture of this kid at the shopping centre. He's got flowers on his shoulders and this lunatic grin on his face as he looks up, and because he's waving this spade in the air (which looks like a weapon the way he's holding it) you have to believe he's going to destroy something. And he's wearing this horrible sweater with a word as big as a bus on the chest. The word is JIGGY. The caption under the photo says:

THE BROOK FARM VANDAL.

DO YOU KNOW THIS BOY?

Hey. Some days you can't win whatever you do.

Jiggy McCue

Turn the page to get a taster
of Jiggy's next outrageously funny
and wildly wacky adventure...

The Killer Underpants

Chapter one

Before we go any further I'd better come clean about my underpants. What I mean is, no one actually died because of them – though there's no telling what would have happened if I'd had to wear them much longer.

I blame my mother. If my mum wasn't such a fanatic about the things you wear next to your skin none of this would have happened. OK, so maybe five weeks is a little long to walk around in a single pair of pants, but I always whip them off at night to give them a shot of oxygen, so what's the big deal? The morning my troubles started I'd just got out of bed and was slotting my trusty old snuggies into place for the day when Mum came in. Well, came in. She flung my door back so hard I almost went out the window.

'Jiggy McCue!' she screeched. 'The state of your underpants!'

'Have you ever heard of knocking?' I said. 'It's that little thing people do with their knuckles before barging into a kid's bedroom.'

'They're disgusting,' she said. 'They're filthy. They're full of holes.'

'Mother,' I said, 'they're meant to have holes. Holes are what underpants do best. Now was there anything else or did you just come in to have a go at my holey underpants?'

'I came in,' she said, 'because I'm sick to death of shouting myself hoarse for you to get up. But now that I've seen the condition of those articles, I see I'm going to have to reorganise my day. I have some shopping to do!'

'Oh no,' I said. 'Not new underpants. You know I hate new underpants. I've told you before, underpants need time to settle in, make themselves at home, breed a little friendly mould and fungus...'

I stopped. What was the point? She was a parent. Worse than that she was a mother. Mothers don't understand these things. They also don't bother to listen half the time. 'And you're coming with me,' she said, to prove it.

'Whoa there,' I said. 'I don't do shopping, remember? Specially with my mother. It's number 47 in the *Book of Rules for Good Parents* I made for you and Dad at Christmas.'

'Put something on over those hideous things, they make me feel quite ill,' she said. 'We leave in ten minutes.'

'Wait!' I cried, skidding on my knees to my chest of drawers. I tore a drawer open, started chucking things over my shoulder. 'I have another pair, I know I have, saw them here only last month. Bingo!' I jumped up, shook my other cosy old pair of holey underpants in her face. 'I'll just change into these, then we don't need to go and buy more – right?'

'Yes, you will change into them,' she said. 'Then I'll at least have the comfort of knowing that if you get knocked down by a bus you'll be in *clean* underwear.'

'No, you miss the point,' I said. 'I mean I'll wear

these *instead* of buying new ones. I'm saving you money. Why throw it away on new ones when I still have a spare pair? OK, Mum? Deal?'

'No,' she said. 'Get changed. Now. We're going to the market!'

And with those nine simple words my fate was sealed. The worst week of my life was about to begin.

Chapter Two

No self-respecting kid wants to be seen shopping with his mother, right? Known fact. Why? Because when you're out shopping with the old dear you always, but always, bump into someone you know, usually just as she's patting your cheek or smoothing your hair down or something. My dad doesn't go a bundle on shopping with Mum either, but at least she keeps her hands off his cheeks and hair.

'Why do I have to tag along?' he whinged the Saturday morning she made us go to the market with her. 'I don't need underpants.'

'You need a new shirt,' she said.

'No I don't. I've already got ten shirts for every day of the week.'

She put on her Deeply Wounded expression. 'Oh, so you don't like the shirts I buy you all of a sudden?'

He panicked. 'No, no, Peg, you buy terrific shirts. But how many do you think a bloke can get through in one lifetime?'

'That's the way I feel about underpants,' I muttered.

My mother stuck her lip out and plunged after it into the market.

The market was pretty crowded. Half my class could be there. I had to keep my wits about me so I could jump away from my mother in a split second. It was OK being seen with Dad. With Dad you don't have to be on your best behaviour, or look presentable, or do your laces up, and he doesn't make you stand still while he holds bits of material against your chest to see if they match your eyes.

Well there we are, Dad and me mooching obediently after the family tyrant, when someone from school comes along — not a kid, but almost as bad.

'Hello,' said Miss Weeks. 'Joseph, isn't it? Joseph McCue?'

'No,' I said.

'It isn't?' she said, surprised because she'd obviously gone to a lot of trouble to memorise the really brilliant kids' names.

'No, Miss, it's Jiggy, Miss. No one calls me Joseph.'

'Why?' she said.

'Because all my life I could never keep still, ever since I was born – and before, according to my mum. She says I almost kicked her to a pulp before she even saw my face.'

She smiled. 'Jiggy it is then. And is this...Mr McCue?'

Dad had stopped traipsing after Mum at the sound of Miss Weeks' voice. Miss Weeks has a nice voice, sort of soft and musical, and she has a nice smile and lots of blonde hair, and when he got an eyeful of her my dad bounced back like a turbo-driven Yo-Yo.

'Call me Mel,' he gushed. 'Short for Melvin, terrible name I know, but I didn't choose it; there's Mel Gibson of course, though I'm taller than him; good weather we're having, how do you do?'

'*Dad!*' I hissed, laying a firm hand on his arm. Did I say it was OK to be seen with my father?

But Miss Weeks wasn't fazed one bit. She just smiled in that nice way she has and stuck her mitt out. 'Erica Weeks. New Deputy Head at Ranting Lane.'

My ex-father went blank. 'Deputy Head?' He

looked at the hand he was suddenly holding. 'Ranting Lane?'

'Your son's school,' Miss Weeks reminded him.

'Oh, that Ranting Lane.' My distant relative shuffled about bashfully, still holding her hand. 'So *you're* the new...hm! Erica, you say?'

'Weeks. Just moved here with my mother.' She glanced about. 'She was with me a minute ago, I seem to have lost her.'

'You can have mine,' I said.

'Hello,' my mother said, appearing out of thin air like an unbottled genie.

The complete stranger known as Dad threw the Deputy Hand away and stuck both of his behind his back to prove they were nothing to do with him. 'This is Emily Leeks,' he said, 'Jiggy's new Heputy Dead.'

Miss Weeks said hello to Mum but didn't stop. 'Must dash. If I don't track down my mother she'll get herself into trouble. Bit eccentric, you know.'

Dad stood watching her go. 'Nice, isn't she?' he said.

'For a Heputy Dead,' Mum said. 'We're in luck. I've found a stall that sells shirts, and right next to it there's a stall that sells underwear.'

'Oh happy day,' I said.

'And this time *do* try and keep up,' she said, and plunged back into the throng. Dad jumped guiltily into line behind her and I got behind him — but not so close people would think I knew them, and we set off once more on our quest for the underpants that were going to make me wish I'd never been born.

Chapter Three

The stall that was about to turn my life into a nightmare looked like something out of a fairground. It was bright red with gold stars all over it and it had a big sign on top which said *Neville's*. It didn't take an Einstein to work out that this was the name of the owner, a dumpy little man in a red bowler hat and yellow waistcoat. He was a real grin-merchant, this Neville, but his grin was one of those insincere switch-on, switch-off types. The sort you buy in joke shops in a packet labelled 'Bad Grin'.

Mum made Dad stand still so she could hold a shirt against him from the stall next door. Then she told him to hold it there himself while she ransacked the underpant section on Neville's stall. Dad knew better than to move, so did the shirt, but I shoved my hands in my pockets to show how cool I was in case anyone saw me. While I hung there this little old biddy in a shawl hobbled by. She caught me giving her the cool once-over before I had a chance to glance elsewhere, and darted towards me.

'Lucky heather? Buy my lucky heather?'

I looked down my nose at this basket of purple stuff she'd stuck under it. 'Heather?' I said. 'What would I want heather for? I mean, like, what would I do with it?'

'Bring you luck,' the ancient crone said. 'Just a coin or two and good luck will follow you wherever you go. Don't you want good luck, young man?'

I chuckled, cucumber cool. 'I make my own luck. Heather? Hey, who needs it?'

'That's a shame,' she said. 'Because great and terrible things are in store for you, and my heather might have protected you from the worst that is to come.'

'Great and terrible things?' I flipped my collar up to cover the hairs that had just stood to attention on the back of my neck.

'I have the Eye,' she said.

'Sorry to hear that,' I said.

'Great and terrible things,' she said again, and then once more, probably for luck: 'Great and terrible things.'

'Hey, this has been nice,' I said. 'Must do it again. Bye now.'

'Beware the very next thing you touch,' the little old woman said.

'I'll do that,' I said, and turned away laughing coolly.

'What do you think of these, Jiggy?' my mother said, thrusting something soft into my hands.

My laugh died. 'Huh?'

'One hundred per cent jersey-cotton. Your size.'

I looked down. I was holding this one hundred per cent jersey-cotton multicoloured horror story against my lower decks.

'Mum. They're horrible.'

'Well you're having them.'

I looked up. It had to be better than looking down. Wrong. I stifled a shriek. My mother's eyes (which were glaring at me) were not their usual bluey-grey colour, they were all red and bulgy. I glanced round for the little old gypsy woman or whatever she was. She'd disappeared. Maybe before she went she'd passed the Eye on to my mother because I'd turned down her lousy lucky heather.

Mum turned to Neville the Badly Grinning Stallholder.

'We'll take these,' she said.

I looked for my dad. A word from the Man of the House might help here, a second opinion which happened to be exactly the same as mine. The Man of the House wasn't there. He'd waited till my mother was concentrating on me, then dumped the shirt and made a run for it – to a pub, knowing him.

'Mu-um,' I said in a whiny little voice. It works sometimes. Not today though. She handed the horrible underpants to Neville, who put them in a bag which unfortunately didn't have a dustbin round it. As he gave the bag to my mother in return for her money, he turned the Bad Grin on me. I shrank back. The way he *looked* at me! Terrifying.

When we got home I was instructed to change into the new pants but take a shower first and get clean, Jiggy, *clean*. So I went to the bathroom, locked the door, turned the shower on, and sat on the toilet reading a comic till I felt enough time had passed. Then I flicked some water at the bath towel to prove I'd used it and unfolded the new underpants.

I didn't like them any better at second glance than at first. They had this swirly-whirly pattern all over them which made your head spin. Even the label was weird. It was on the outside, on the front − and *printed* back-to-front. I didn't bother straining my brain trying to read the thing, but I made a vow to keep away from buses. Tyre tracks might improve these things a little, but I wouldn't be caught dead in them, even to please my mother.

With a heavy sigh I stepped into the new underpants. Right foot, left foot, then the big upward haul, bend the knees for the last little lift, wriggle the hips to introduce them to the hardware, and there they were, home.

But then something happened. Something that doesn't usually happen when you put new undies on. They shrank to fit. True. They did. Gave the personal places a sort of hello hug and forgot to let go. I felt like a cling-filmed fruit bowl.

But it was at bedtime that I began to realise I had a problem on my hands. Well, not my hands exactly, but you know what I mean. I was stripping off to jump into my PJs and catch the fast train to Dreamworld, and everything went smoothly enough till I got down to the pants. They wouldn't budge. They absolutely refused to drop, or even droop, no matter how hard I tugged. My blinding new underpants with the dyslexic designer label clung to me like a second skin.

A second skin that wouldn't come off.

You'll have to read the rest of
The Killer Underpants
to find out what happens next...

1 84121 713 1   £4.99

The underpants from hell – that's what Jiggy
calls them, and not just because they look so
gross. No, these pants are evil. And they're
in control. Of him. Of his life!
Can Jiggy get to the bottom of his problem
before it's too late?

*Join Jiggy McCue and his pals Pete and Angie
in this pant-tastically funny adventure!*

Stockton Children's Book of the Year Shortlisted

1 84121 752 2   £4.99

Feel like your life has gone down the pan?
Well here's your chance to swap it
for a better one!

When those tempting words appear on the
computer screen, Jiggy McCue just can't resist.
He hits "F for Flush" and... Oh dear.
He really shouldn't have done that. Because
the life he gets in place of his own is a very
embarrassing one – for a boy.

Another loo-ny adventure with Jiggy and
The Three Musketeers!

Michael Lawrence

1 84121 756 5   £4.99

Jiggy McCue is the unluckiest kid in town.
He wants some good luck for a change.
But instead of luck he gets a genie.
A teenage genie who turns against him.
Then the maggoty dreams start.
Dreams which, with his luck and this
genie, might just come true.

*Go on, flick the pages for
a maggoty mouthful!*

orchard Red Apples

Orchard Red Apples are available from all good bookshops,
or can be ordered direct from the publisher:
Orchard Books, PO BOX 29, Douglas IM99 1BQ
Credit card orders please telephone 01624 836000
or fax 01624 837033 or visit our Internet site: www.wattspub.co.uk
or e-mail: bookshop@enterprise.net for details.

To order please quote title, author and ISBN
and your full name and address.
Cheques and postal orders should be made payable to
'Bookpost plc.'
Postage and packing is FREE within the UK
(overseas customers should add £1.00 per book).
Prices and availability are subject to change.

What they say about The Poltergoose

HONK!

I would give this book 10 out of 10
Victoria Guilder, age 9

A Laugh a Minute, I couldn't stop turning the pages!
Caroline Holworthy, age 12

I thought this book was excellent, the exciting storyline, the perfect description of the things the goose did and the results.
Carolyn Thomas, age 11

I would recommend this to anybody
Simon Ward

The Poltergoose is brilliant!
Sarah Goddard, age 10

A clever, funny story which children will be able to relate to
Alison Broderick, age 11

HONK!

Hilarious.
Times Educational Supplement

The Poltergoose is full of detail and a brilliant book
Mark Middleton

Rib-tickling.
Sunderland Echo

wacky and streetwise.
The Bookseller

I liked the comical storyline
Victoria Walton, age 12

HONK!

What they say about
The Killer Underpants

Hilarious.
The Independent

"A good book to read and it will make you laugh."
Kirsty Irwin
YARN

Has irresistible boy appeal.
The Bookseller

Entertaining and original
Booktrust

"The story really made me giggle. A brilliant book to read for everyone!"
Rebecca Moss
Acquila

"Some very funny things happen in this book. It made me laugh out loud."
Elizabeth Law
YARN

This is the funniest book I've ever read.
Teen Titles

Quirky, cheeky fun that children will love.
Books Magazine/
Publishing News